In the Still of the Night

In the Still of the Night

Night

Tales to Lock Your Doors By

Dorothy Salisbury Davis

Five Star
Unity, Maine

Five Star First Edition Mystery Series.
Published in 2001 in conjunction with
Tekno Books and Ed Gorman.

Cover design by Carol Pringle.

Set in 11 pt. Plantin by Al Chase.

Printed in the United States on permanent paper.

Library of Congress Cataloging-in-Publication Data
Davis, Dorothy Salisbury.
    In the still of the night : tales to lock your doors by /
Dorothy Salisbury Davis.
        p.   cm.
    Contents: To forget Mary Ellen—Now is forever—The
puppet—Justina—Christopher and Maggie—The scream
—Till death do us part—Miles to go.
    ISBN 0-7862-3007-X (hc : alk. paper)
    1. Detective and mystery stories, American.   I. Title.
PS3554.A9335 I5 2001
813'.54—dc21   00-051067

Table of Contents

To Forget Mary Ellen

The two men sat in Gibbons's 1990 Ford Taurus in the parking lot of Freddie's Diner on the West Side of Manhattan. In November it was already dark at five-thirty. Everyone on the street, except the homeless, was bucking the wind, homeward bound. The two men were unnoticed.

Joseph (Red) Gibbons was a retired New York detective. The subject of unproven charges of corruption and misconduct, he'd been given early retirement several years before. It was widely suspected also that he abused his wife, but Mary Ellen simply would not swear out a complaint against him. He was an affable man most of the time, generous, with a glib tongue and a ready handshake. He was also a bully, and it came out when anyone of lower rank crossed him, or when he'd had a few drinks, or, unpredictably, with his wife.

Billy Phillips was crouched down on the passenger side. The round-shouldered Phillips had crouched so much of his life it was his natural posture. On the move he was quick and simian; huddled in a chair or a car seat he had very nearly the inanimacy of a rag doll. In the neighborhood he was thought to be a kind man, he was very good to Marge, his wife, and he adored their ten-year-old son, William. There were rumors that he was connected with the Rooney Gang, but nobody suspected in what capacity. Some said it had to do with gambling. Phillips was a hit man, a paid killer. His wife took for granted that they lived on the horses and what she earned as a hairdresser in a neighborhood beauty salon. Billy was a good handicapper and every once in a while took off without notice

7

for a few days at whatever track was in operation at that time of year.

Gibbons and Phillips had met only once before, when Gibbons was still a working detective. Phillips had made a rare slip-up: he had left evidence that would eventually incriminate him on the scene. Rooney had told him he might get lucky, Gibbons was on the case. By appointment he had gone to Gibbons's home, a loft in the West Thirties, and Mrs. Gibbons, Mary Ellen, had opened the loft door to him, not even curious about how he got into the building. He wouldn't have told her the truth anyway. He observed an ugly bruise on her cheek, but he recognized her as a battered woman more from the wary look in her eyes, the hang of her head, the sloping shoulders, especially the shoulders. The slope had particular meaning to him—it recalled his attempts to diminish himself, to become invisible if possible, in childhood, to slip under the blows aimed at him by a runaway father whenever he was coaxed home by the parish priest. Billy Phillips had never laid a hand on his own son, even in just punishment.

The night he had gone to Gibbons's home he was prepared to mortgage his life to get the incriminating evidence back in his own hands or destroyed. He represented himself to Gibbons as an intermediary, the messenger for a friend in trouble. He spoke as an outsider, even though he knew deep down that Gibbons did not believe for a minute he was there on behalf of anyone other than himself. No promises had been given. Both men realized, despite Phillips's sham, that they were prisoners to each other whether or not any word of commitment passed between them.

A few months after that Gibbons was retired. The evidence Phillips was concerned about never surfaced. The case, like his other homicides, remained open, but inactive.

The police lacked both time and new evidence. His success was attributed in part at least to his never using the same weapon twice. After making a hit he took the weapon at once to Fitz Fitzgerald, a gun fence with an overseas outlet. When he needed a safe replacement Fitzgerald always came through for him.

Phillips had a beer now and then in McGowen's Pub on Eighth Avenue and he had seen Gibbons there a few times. They had made eye contact, but that was all. They'd not spoken again until the phone call from Gibbons that set up their meeting in the parking lot of Freddie's Diner.

Phillips appeared, as out of nowhere, got into the car and closed the car door almost soundlessly.

"Been waiting all this time to hear from me?" Gibbons asked him.

"I had a little package ready for you, but I didn't hear so I figured I'd better wait."

"Five years?"

"I thought maybe you'd forgot about it. Maybe you wanted to forget it."

"Cops and elephants don't forget. How big was the little package?"

Phillips shrugged. "I'm not a rich man."

"Maybe you're in the wrong business." Gibbons gave a snort of laughter.

Phillips didn't say anything. He felt like a mouse under the cat's paw.

"When the P.D. put me out to pasture, I went into the in-surance business," the retired cop said. "I had a couple of good years in there before things dried up. I've got what my old lady calls a gift of the gab. It worked miracles when there was money around. The way things are now, half my clients can't pay their premiums. I can hardly pay my own . . ."

The more Gibbons talked about himself, the more uneasy Phillips felt. Why was he supposed to give a damn what Gibbons was doing? He was being set up for something and it was going to come like a kick in the groin. Was the old evidence still around? Was the case going to open again? Gibbons sure as hell wasn't trying to sell him life insurance. But it had to have something to do with insurance. That made him even more nervous. Insurance companies had their own detectives. He pulled in tighter on himself, pushing back on the cushion, down on the seat as though he could disappear into the upholstery.

Gibbons continued, "Want to know what all this bullshit's about?"

"I want to know what size package you're thinking of, yeah."

The ex-cop chortled. "You've got it all wrong, my friend. It was you mentioned the package, not me. I've got a job for you, Phillips, something in your line."

He ought to have known, probably did. Only he didn't want to admit it. He didn't want the job, not for Gibbons. But he was afraid to say so. "You know how I make a buck these days? I handicap horses—all over the country. I guess you knew that, huh?"

"Twenty thousand," Gibbons said, ignoring Phillips's attempt to head him off. "Five when we shake hands, five when the job's done, and ten two years later. We can set the date."

Phillips bit his tongue. It was enough money to choke a horse. His instant calculations ran to where it would be safe to invest it, and how much it would grow to by the time William was old enough for college. It happened to him every time there was a possibility of real money. "What's the two year business?"

"Two years minimum. We're talking insurance. They

don't pay till they can't get out of it. They want absolute proof whatever the claimant says happened did happen. We can handle that. We can see it happens the right way."

Phillips thought he had it now: proof that the deceased died by the rules set down in the policy fine print. Gibbons had got himself named beneficiary of some old Bridget or Norah he'd charmed with his Irish gab. Now he was ready to pull the plug on her. It had to look like a break-in or a street crime. High risk and tricky as hell. Twenty thousand wasn't all that much money.

But he said, "Tell me about it."

"I couldn't do that, Billy, without a commitment from you."

"I can't give you a commitment till I know what I'm getting into. Who? Where? How much time have I got?"

"I'll be working with you all the way."

Phillips was suddenly wary for another reason: Gibbons could be undercover, working for the cops again. He could've got religion. "I work alone," he said. "It's done my way or it ain't done by me."

"I buy that," Gibbons said, "but you might feel different in this case." The lights of a passing car flashed across his face. They caught the screwed-up eyes, the smug grin on his pudgy face.

"I do every case different," Phillips said, "but they all come out the same. See what I mean?"

"Whoever you take a contract on, they're dead. Is that what you're saying? What in hell would I be doing here if I didn't know that?"

"What's the job?"

"I want you to kill my wife."

Phillips wasn't prepared for that one, but he should've been, he thought: Gibbons the wife beater. He had an instant memory of the battered woman who opened the door to him that night five years ago. Gibbons would be working with him all the way. He believed him. And he hated him. Not that he'd loved any bastard he had ever done a job for. "I never did a woman," he growled.

"You know the sign in the window of the beauty shop where your wife works—UNISEX? Look at it that way."

The son of a bitch.

They met the next night two hours later in the same place. Freddie closed early. His main business came at noon from workers in nearby industry and warehouses. A few neighborhood stragglers hardly made it worthwhile to serve evening meals. By eight o'clock the only cars left in the lot would stay overnight. Freddie paid half his rent that way. Gibbons was one of his regulars, familiar to anyone who observed his comings and goings. No one did that night. Phillips considered himself invisible. He'd worked at it long enough, a master of every detail of misguidance. Even Gibbons didn't see him until he opened the car door and slipped in.

"I was thinking," Gibbons started, "you might want to come up to my place and look over the setup. She's home most of the time except on card party nights, but I don't see what difference it makes whether she's home or not. Except on the big night, of course."

"The big night," Phillips repeated.

"Yeah." After a few seconds Gibbons said, "Ever have anyone hang on to you, Phillips? The more you shake them off the tighter they hang on. She's like that. When I can't stand it anymore I let her have it, and you know, the poor girl likes it? When I get over the rage, see, I'm sorry. Then she's all over me. Do this to me, do that. I go out of there hollering. If I didn't, I'd kill her."

"So why don't you?"

12

"Don't be a smart-ass," Gibbons said.

"You're still living in the same place?" Phillips asked.

"Same loft, same wife, same stinking elevator. You'll have to watch that."

Phillips had no intention of going near an elevator. Elevators were traps. If there weren't stairs . . . but he knew there were. He'd used them the one time he'd been there. He said nothing, however. He'd hear Gibbons out. He did things his way, but that wasn't to say it couldn't be changed to suit the circumstances.

"I got to tell you, we've been broken into twice. That's how I got the idea. I scared them off once. Next time I wasn't there. They beat up on Mary Ellen . . . Messed the place up. I figured it's a good idea for us to mess things up, too."

Us, Phillips noted.

"I could do it myself when I get there," Gibbons reconsidered. "No, better not. You never know how you'll feel when the time comes. We've been married thirty years, you know. If we'd had kids everything might have been different."

Yeah, you'd beat up on the kids, Phillips thought. He twisted in his seat. The family talk was making him nervous. "Let's stick to business, okay? Let's hear your game plan and I'll tell you if it'll work."

"It's so simple, it's scary. The first two floors in my building's industrial, see—in by eight A.M., out at five. I've got the fifth floor, right? I've been there fifteen years. But the owner's turning the third and fourth floor into apartments. More bucks. All these classy apartments are ready. But they can't get occupancy certificates. The plumbing's fucked up. A few hundred bucks under the table, no problem. But it's not my business. The thing is, after quitting time there's nobody, but nobody, in the building."

There was never nobody, by Phillips's reckoning, but he

said, "Okay, let's have the rest of it."

"A couple of nights a week I'm in the habit of staying out late. I don't stay over, but I stay plenty late. She knows where I am but I call her anyway, especially since the break-in. I got a downstairs key for you. You'll have to get rid of it good."

"I don't want your key," Phillips said.

"The night we settle on, you'll be in the hall outside the door when I phone. I'll let you know the time I'm going to call her and you'll wait a couple of minutes after you hear the phone ring. Then you'll ring the doorbell. Maybe knock and ring at the same time. The bell doesn't always work. I'll tell her to find out who it is, and when she calls out to you, you'll say it's Sergeant Nichols from the precinct. You brought a package 'round for me." Gibbons laughed. "That little package keeps turning up, don't it? Fact is, that's what happens once in a while. I'll tell her to open the door and it'll be that simple."

"Nothing is ever that simple," Phillips growled.

"But we can work 'round it?"

"Suppose I can't make it on target, or something gets in the way, like the real Sergeant Nichols?"

"There is no Sergeant Nichols. Then we start over another time. If you're not there she can't let you in, can she?"

"Have you got a revolver, Sergeant?"

"I've got my service .38. I was damn glad to break it out the night of the attempted robbery."

"What if your wife has it in her hand when she comes to the door?"

"She can't. I took it over to the office last week when things got uptight between her and me."

"Think she'd kill you if she got the chance?"

"Hell no. I was scared she might kill herself."

Stupid-head me, Phillips thought. Insurance companies

14

didn't pay off on suicides. "I want that gun," he said.

"The hell you do. It's got my name all over it. I had to register it at the precinct when I retired."

"The weapon's no problem, but I want that one. I'll tell you why. This is how it's got to play to Homicide: No phone call. Let them figure out why she opens the door. You've told her time and again not to, right? So when she opens it, she comes on with your revolver—" Gibbons tried to interrupt. "Listen to what I'm saying. She comes on with the gun. The guy outside the door knocks it out of her hand. Maybe she gets shot in the scuffle. The cops can figure that out, too. That's how it's got to play to Homicide. In real life the shooter hangs up the phone before he leaves the premises. That way you know it came out like it was planned. Is there a witness on your end of the phone?"

"There won't be."

"You won't have to mess up the apartment. The shooter's got the piece. To him it's worth the kill."

"I want to think about it," Gibbons said. "That gun's like my right arm."

What bothered Phillips more than anything else about the job was his hatred of Gibbons. He didn't like working inside a building. He'd take fences over walls any day. And he didn't like it that the contract was on a woman. But every time he thought of Gibbons it was like something started crawling inside him. He could see his puffy face, his screwed-up eyes. And he knew that if ever he saw this man lay his hand on the wife he'd go berserk. It was like that when he saw anybody knocking a kid around. He'd almost got arrested once in a supermarket when he caught hold of a woman and pulled her away from where she was slapping the kid in its stroller. He didn't want to think too much about Mary Ellen. Where the hell was women's lib? She'd be better off dead, he told him-

15

self, than spoiling her life with Gibbons. But there was the twenty thousand dollars. The most he ever got for a hit was five grand.

The final meeting before the hit date occurred at Gibbons's loft. Mary Ellen played cards every other Wednesday night at the church hall. Gibbons would go over to McGowen's Pub for a few beers and then pick her up on his way home. When he told her he was staying home that night, that he didn't feel so great, she wanted to skip the card game. But when he blew up at her for it, she took off. He called after her that he'd pick her up as usual.

Phillips was watching from across the street. There wasn't much traffic, most of it the precinct cops taking in the whores from Eleventh Avenue and the crosstown Thirties: sweep night. There were night-lights on all the floors of Gibbons's building—pale, low-wattage bulbs you'd think would die any minute. And he couldn't see a homeless slob on the street, the cleanest street in town. Real treacherous. Gibbons's wife left the building at ten minutes to eight. He wasn't sure at first that it was her, the way she walked with her head up, her shoulders back, a tote bag swinging at her side. Good legs and noisy heels. It had to be her. The time was right and nobody else came out of the building. He could hear the clack of her heels far down the street.

That night he got into the vestibule the way everybody else did, by ringing Gibbons's bell and waiting to be buzzed in. He even took the elevator to the fifth floor. Never again. It climbed one floor after another as though it wouldn't make the next. Gibbons was waiting for him in the hallway. "Did you see her?"

"It must've been her. Nobody else came out of the building."

"I don't pick her up till ten, but I'd like to get you out of

16

here as soon as we get things settled."

"Suits me."

"Want a drink?"

Phillips shook his head. "Let's get on with it." He sat down on a straight chair, having hooked it out with his foot from the round polished table. Mary Ellen kept a bare and tidy house. No plants, a couple of holy pictures. He thought about all the room there was in a loft. William, raised in a railroad flat, would go wild in a place like this. Phillips's nerves began to jump, the tension grabbed at the back of his neck when Gibbons returned.

"Fifty C-notes," Gibbons said, and took a packet of mixed old and new bills from a paper bag. "Want to count them?"

"You do it for me," Phillips said.

Gibbons put the already heavy bag down carefully on the table, removed the rubber band from the bills and slipped it onto his wrist. He counted the bills aloud, stacking them by tens on the table. "Satisfied?"

Phillips stood up and took his wallet from his slacks pocket. "Give me twenty of them." He stuffed them into the wallet and put it away. "Put the band back on the rest of them." He put the packet into his breast pocket.

They confirmed the date of the hit and the date and place of the final payoff. Phillips sat down again and they went through the setup one last time. Phillips looked around at the phone where it sat on a table between two easy chairs that faced the television set.

"What about the bedroom phone?"

"I told you, it's on a jack that's broke. I'm supposed to fix it but I won't."

Phillips got to his feet. A wall clock with one of those sunshine faces showed a quarter to nine. He motioned to the paper bag. "Let's have it."

"Take it."

"I don't want the bag. Hand me the gun."

"Goddamn it, take it yourself." The sweat glistened on Gibbons's forehead.

Seeing Gibbons sweat was balm to Phillips's nerves. "It's clean, right?" He reached into the bag and brought out the .38 police revolver. Beautiful. It looked as new as the day it came from the gunsmith. He flicked off the safety and rolled the cylinder. Every chamber was loaded. He reset the safety. "Thanks for the spares," he said. "Got any more?"

Gibbons sucked in his breath and let it out. "The rest of the box. It's on the closet shelf in the shoe box."

"Leave it there." Phillips put the gun in the pocket of his jacket, kneed his chair back into place, and went to the door. He looked back. Gibbons was still standing at the table, crumpling the bag, staring after him. He was shaking, Phillips realized. Gibbons was scared shitless. The stinking coward was scared of him. Phillips knew himself the man had good reason. "Let me out of here, will you?" he said.

Gibbons moved with a start. He tossed the bag on the table and strode to the door.

In the hall Phillips turned back. Gibbons stuck out his hand. They had never shaken hands, and didn't then. Phillips made his hit face to face with his victim for the first time ever.

Nothing this night had gone the way Mary Ellen expected it to. She had left the house in a rage of her own and vented some of it clattering down the street. Like all her rages, it turned in on herself. She knew there was something wrong with her to take all the abuse she got from Red. It was sick to love him even more afterwards. At one time they'd taken counseling together from their parish priest. Red had insisted on it. The gist of what the priest had to say was, "Why don't you fight back, Mary Ellen?" "I wish to God she would," Red told the priest. But when she tried it with about as much punch as a kitten's paw, he'd twisted her arm behind her and said, "Don't you ever try that again."

She knew he was having an affair and she'd left the house convinced the woman would arrive at the loft as soon as she was safely out of the way. When Red blew up because she decided to stay home with him, she felt absolutely certain. She could taste the pain and pleasure of knowing them to be in bed together—in her bed. Her mind was on fire with the thought of actually seeing it. Give them enough time and then go back quietly. She tried to concentrate on the card game at first. Red would kill her. But she didn't really care. When an extra player showed up at the card game she gladly gave up her place. At twenty past eight she started back home, at half-past eight she left the elevator on the fourth floor and walked up the one flight of fire stairs. Before she even got near the loft door she heard the voices, Red's and another man's. She fled, ashamed and panicky. Red would kill her if he knew she'd come home, and he'd know why she did the minute she tried to lie about it. She got all the way back to the door of the parish hall and heard the scrape of chairs, the talk and laughter as the switch in bridge partners took place. She had no heart for the game and there wasn't a place for her anyway. There really wasn't a place for her anywhere. She felt ashamed, disappointed, crazy.

Whether suicide entered her mind she was never going to be able to say for sure, but she walked to the river, past the air force carrier *Intrepid* in its semi-permanent dock, and through the scattered people out on a chilly weeknight. She walked out on the long pier. Some way along it and close to the water's edge, she found herself among materials set out for dock repair: the barricade had been overturned, the lantern an askew red eye. Backing out she sank her heel into a glob of tar. She pulled her shoe out and tried to remove the gummy residue with Kleenex, then with an emery board, finally with the nail polish remover she had in her tote bag. She only made things worse. The only place to deal with it was at home. She checked her watch under the first high-density streetlight.

She avoided passing the church hall where Red would soon be turning up to walk her home. If she hurried she could get to the loft well ahead of him. She might not have time to clean the shoe, but she could hide it away and not have to confess that part of the night's silliness. And she'd pretend she hadn't heard him say he would pick her up as usual. She took off her shoes and ran the last part of the way home.

Homicide Detective John Moran and his partner Al Russo took Mary Ellen and her lawyer back to the loft at seven in the morning. She had been questioned throughout the night at precinct headquarters. The lawyer, a smart young fellow recommended by Moran himself, demanded that the police charge her or release her. Moran was, to the extent his duty allowed, on Mary Ellen's side. He had known Gibbons when he was on the force; he knew him for a smiling Irishman with a cruel streak in him, a lot of charm until it wasn't working. Then he was a son of a bitch. He knew that Gibbons abused his wife. A jury might come out on her side, too, but it would go better for her if she confessed, let her lawyer spell out what a bastard her husband was. And it would be better for Moran himself if he could break the case now, before the brass moved in.

He was dog-tired and well into overtime. His partner was asleep on his feet and the suspect was a staggering zombie, but Moran was determined on one more go-round with her. It might be irregular to bring her back to the scene so soon, but he got away with it. He wanted her to see the forensic crew still at work, the scraping and the measuring, the chalked outline of the figure who had lain there. She had been fingerprinted and tested for powder burns. None showed up, but the tar and the polish remover rendered the findings inconclusive. If she was guilty the whole tar and tar removal bit could have been calculated. The long pier had been checked out and at dawn a diving team was scheduled to search the river along the pilings for the gun. She readily admitted knowing there was a revolver in the house. It had been there for years. But she could not account for why it was missing now—unless her husband had taken it to his office. Or the man she'd heard him talking to had got it from him. The last time she had seen it was the night of the break-in when her husband scared off the burglars. The medical examiner had not yet offered any findings on the spent cartridge.

They went through the CRIME SCENE barricade in the first daylight. People on their way to work were routed away from the building and got no more out of the uniformed cops than that a police investigation was going on. But the rumors had it about right and a *Daily News* photographer was on hand. The minute he started shooting pictures the word went up, "That's her! That's the wife!"

Moran began what he hoped was the final grilling inside the entrance to the building. He wanted to know where the elevator was when she rang for it.

Mary Ellen swayed, a little dizzy when she looked up at the floor indicator. Her lawyer offered his arm. She threw it off. She was home and that was support enough for now. "It was on the fifth floor. That's what made me even surer she was up there."

"You took the elevator to the fourth floor yourself. Why not the fifth?"

"I didn't want them to hear it stop on our floor."

"But wouldn't they have heard it starting down for you? Or wasn't it right there waiting on the first floor, where you'd left it when you went out?"

"I've told you the truth. Are you trying to trap me?"

"I'm trying to help you," Moran said. "I don't know that there was a man up there at all unless you convince me there was."

"I heard him. That's all I can tell you."

"Were they arguing? Were they laughing? Come on, lady, you heard something. What was it?"

"Just voices. They were talking."

"Voices make words. That's how people communicate. Didn't you hear one word?"

She shook her head and swayed again.

The lawyer said, "Mrs. Gibbons needs to sit down, sir."

"So do the rest of us," Moran snapped. He pressed the button and the elevator door slid open noisily.

Mary Ellen did not allow herself to see that which she did not want to see. She was aware of men at work, the hallway filled with equipment, cigarette smoke, light that was blinding. She longed to be inside the loft with everything else shut out. She fought off the memory of that other return. Over the years she had rehearsed a like scene many times when Red was on the force. She clutched her lawyer's arm and looked only at the ceiling while they edged their way around the floor tape. Moran allowed her to use the bathroom, given the all-clear by the crew.

There were only three rooms to the loft, the bedroom, the kitchen, and the very large living room. The round table with its four chairs had been dusted for prints. It was available to them. Moran seated the group the way he wanted them, allowing Mrs. Gibbons to keep her back to the area under investigation. If he wanted to make her look there, he could. At the moment he wanted her cooperation, not her collapse. He resumed his questioning; Russo activated a small tape recorder.

"Suppose, just for a minute, Mrs. Gibbons, you had not heard those voices, what would you have done?"

"I'd've let myself in real quiet. If there wasn't a light on in the big room—that's what we call this room, the big room—if there wasn't a light on here, I'd have sneaked through and turned on the light switch to the bedroom just as I opened the door."

"How would you have felt if there was no one there?"

"Don't answer that," the lawyer intervened.

"You'd have been disappointed, right?" Moran amended.

"I was disappointed when I heard those voices. Oh, yes. I wanted her to be there with him, if that's what you want me to say."

"All I want you to say is the truth." Moran drew a deep, raspy breath. He wanted a cigarette, but he'd smoked his last one before leaving headquarters. "Let me tell it the way I see it, Mrs. Gibbons. You were absolutely sure you'd catch them here last night if you came back early. In your bed! In *your* bed. So when you got the chance early in the evening, you took the revolver from the closet shelf, from a shoe box, right? And tucked it into that bag of yours. Lots of room. No problem." He paused. She was shaking her head. "So what's wrong with it?"

"I'd've been scared Red would catch me taking it."

"Was he home *all* the time? Didn't step out for cigarettes, a breath of air? Didn't get a telephone call that kept him on the line—a call from his other woman, let's say, so he'd be glad to see you disappear in the bedroom?"

"You're wrong, wrong, wrong. That just didn't happen." She put her head down on her arms on the table.

Moran tucked his hand under her chin and forced her head up. His face close to her, he said, "Let's go back to the question. If you didn't hear those voices, what would you have done?"

"I told you I'd have sneaked in."

Moran interrupted. "And if you'd found them in bed, naked as baboons, making love so hot you could smell it?"

Her whole forlorn expression changed. She smiled, her dead eyes caught fire. "Yes!" she cried encouragingly. "Yes!"

Christ, Moran thought, she's enjoying this.

When the medical examiner agreed that the fatal bullet had probably come from the box of cartridges found on the shelf of Gibbons's closet, pressure mounted within and outside the police department for the arrest of Mary Ellen Gibbons. The insurance representatives kept to the background, but the company made it plain they wanted to see a case developed along the lines of murder for profit, the direction toward which the district attorney's office was already inclined. While Gibbons had written the policy and paid its premiums by pouring virtually all his commissions into it, Mary Ellen was co-signatory. Indeed their investments and bank accounts were in both names. The only noticeable irregularity in the Gibbons's finances was that in the past eighteen months he had, on several occasions, failed to deposit their monthly dividend check from mutual funds. This, however, coincided with his extramarital affair with a woman who testified to "his generous care of her."

As for physical evidence, the weapon itself had not been

found. Given the tides, the muck, and the undertow of the Hudson River, this was not surprising. The grappling for it went on. None of the fingerprints brought up in the Gibbons home indicated a visitor that night. There were simply no witnesses to confirm that part of Mary Ellen's story. Testimony to her erratic behavior was ample. Her distracted behavior at the card party was readily testified to, as was the hour at which she cut out of the game. A young couple came forward who had seen her bumbling around the pier repair site. They were afraid she might fall or jump into the river and turned back themselves, not to be involved. They had intended to report her to the first cop they encountered, but by the time they came on one they decided that their imagination had exaggerated her strange behavior.

Mary Ellen never wavered in her account of that night's activities. She admitted that although she had known of her husband's affair for a year, and had found out where the woman lived, she had not until that night tried to confront them. Detective Moran tried to believe, along with almost everyone on the case, that she had contrived the story to cover the murder of her husband. But he could not reconcile her responses under questioning with murder for profit. He was superseded in the case, not taken off it, but dropped down a couple of notches in authority. The Police Benevolent Association was adding pressure: one of their own had been murdered.

Her arrest, Moran knew, was imminent. Without quite realizing how it happened, he found himself back where he had started, on Mary Ellen's side. As he said to Al Russo, who had answered the complaint with him that night, "You saw that place—all the comforts of a zoo. That money wouldn't mean much to her if she was to get it."

"Wait till the lawyer's bills come in. She'll need it then."

Moran thought about what Russo said. It was out of sync. And that was what he felt about the whole case. The money angle would make sense if Mary Ellen was the victim, her husband the one to profit from her death. No one would pay those premiums without expecting to collect. That's what made it crazy: he paid the premiums. He had to believe she was going to die first. And here she was, about to be charged with his murder, frozen into a story she hadn't moved a shadow's length away from.

On Saturday morning Moran went over the prints again. It was the third day after the homicide. Most of the recent prints had been identified, including those of Mary Ellen's sister—whom she was staying with now—and a plumber. Moran studied Gibbons's prints on the table. Those marked FRESH were in one place where, he figured out, Gibbons would have been facing the door. He got out the crime scene photos of the table and chairs. He was a few seconds identifying the one item on the table.

It was a crumpled paper bag. His association was instantaneous. Now. Not originally. The bag had gone to the lab. It would take time to bring up prints on the rough paper. Moran tore through the transcripts of Mary Ellen's statements— when questioned she did not remember the paper bag at all. Her husband might have gone out after she left the house, but not before it. Moran turned to the autopsy report: there had been no food intake after that night's early dinner. Gibbons did not smoke. The inventory of personal effects showed his wallet to have contained ninety-eight dollars. It was still in his pocket when he was shot. Eighty cents in change had spilled out on the floor. Moran turned everything around and made himself assume Mary Ellen to be telling the truth. The paper bag fit the payoff tradition. Someone had come to the loft with it, or for it? The man whose voice Mary Ellen claimed to have heard was real. He had been there. So what went wrong between him and Gibbons? If they'd been quarreling she'd have known that much at least from the pitch of their voices.

Moran went back to the monthly dividend checks Gibbons had failed to deposit. They totaled $5,100. But something else showed up: Mary Ellen was not as ignorant of their finances as he had supposed. On several occasions she had requested a bank printout of their accounts. So she would have been aware that Gibbons was siphoning off the occasional dividend check. She *could* have been aware. Was it one more example of her masochism to have known and been silent?

Yet another possibility occurred to the detective. Suppose a killer hired by Gibbons had gone to her and told her he was being paid $5,000, say, to kill her. Say he asked her to make it ten and he would turn the gun on Gibbons. Would she finally, finally, have taken the offense against her husband and said, "Go ahead. Kill the bastard!"?

Phillips had run down the four flights of stairs that night knowing he should have gone back into the apartment and taken the paper bag. But too much blood had spattered and there was too little time. When Gibbons failed to pick her up at ten she'd come home on her own. Poor sick woman, he had done her a good turn and he hoped she'd appreciate it some time. Now he had to forget Mary Ellen and make new plans for himself.

On the street he stood a moment sucking in the air to clear his head of the reek of gunpowder. His hearing was coming back. A noisy argument was building mid-block. The cops would be close at hand when Mary Ellen wanted them. He went the other way and set himself an ambling gait with little simian spurts now and then. If anyone noticed him at all in the twenty blocks uptown and the two long blocks west, he'd be taken for a harmless drunk. In fact, he picked up an empty wine bottle, discarded it, and kept the brown bag it was wrapped in. He worked the revolver into the bag without taking it from his pocket.

It wasn't ten o'clock yet when he reached Mickey's Place, the hangout of the Rooneys. Rooney was out of town, Phillips was glad to hear. Fitz Fitzgerald was the one he wanted to see, without Rooney putting his nose in. Fitz was shooting pool. He had three more balls to clear the table. Phillips went into the back room, called the "conference room," and waited for him. He tried to remember the names of the former gang members whose initials were carved in the table. Fitzgerald came in flushed with a win. He looked scrubbed and, as usual, wore a white shirt and striped tie. He looked like a bank teller, and his daytime job wasn't far from that mark: he worked in a check-cashing shop. He looked no more like a gun fence than Phillips looked like a killer. The first thing he asked was if the gun was hot.

"Plenty. You don't get it unless you got a place for it outside the U.S.A. And I don't mean Ireland."

"You know I ain't political, Billy. Let's have a look at it and you can tell me how much you want."

"Half what you can get for it, and I'm willing to wait for mine." He slipped the gun from the bag.

Fitzgerald's face went white. He knew a police special when he saw one. He began to back off.

"It's okay with me if you put it on ice for a while," Phillips cajoled. "I'm going out to the West Coast tracks in the morning. Just put it on ice and I'll check with you at the end of the week."

Fitzgerald moistened his lips. "Rooney won't like it, Billy. He keeps saying, 'Some of my best friends—' "

Phillips cut in, "Does he have to find out? It's you and me doing business here."

"He finds out most things, don't he?"

"Yeah, when some fink tells him."

"I ain't no fink and you know it, Billy."

"What in hell would I be doing here if I didn't know that?"

The words had a familiar ring: it was what Gibbons had said talking him into the job.

Marge Phillips was about to leave the house on Saturday morning when the phone rang. She hoped her perm customer wasn't canceling.

"Is Billy back yet?"

"He's not, but he's due in around noon."

"It's Fitz Fitzgerald, Marge. I got to deliver a package to Billy and it's got to be this morning, Rooney's orders. Could I bring it around to you on my way to the shop?"

"Ah, Fitz, I won't be here, but William's home. I'll have him watch out the window for you. It'll give him something to do and keep him out of mischief till his father gets here."

Fitzgerald hesitated. "The kid wouldn't open it, would he?"

"Not if you tell him he mustn't. He's very good that way."

Moran was in the squad room unwrapping his lunch when the report came through of a ten-year-old boy dead on arrival at Roosevelt Hospital. He'd been shot while playing with a .38 revolver. Moran stuck the sandwich in his pocket on his way to the desk. "I want to roll on this one, Sergeant. I'm looking for a .38. Maybe I'll get lucky."

Now Is Forever

They met in the Medieval Sculpture Hall of the Metropolitan Museum of Art. It is a vast room through which museum visitors can go off in any of several directions—to galleries for special exhibits, into the wing housing the Lehman Collection, through the Medieval Treasury and on to the Garden Court and the American Wing. It is so vast a room one almost always feels alone, no matter how numerous the company. They shook hands and spoke softly, words that any listener, picking up on them, might interpret as casual. It looked like, and was contrived to look like, an accidental meeting after which, as though there were a discovery she had made recently and wanted to show him, they moved into the small Romanesque chapel with its thirteenth-century stained glass. They stared up at the window from the Lady Chapel of the Abbey of St. Germain des Prés, not really seeing it. They were too absorbed, too overwhelmed by the sudden presence of one another. But when he reached out and touched her hand where it lay on the back of a chapel chair, she withdrew it, and slowly looked around toward a wood carving of mother and child. Beyond the sculpture she could see the hall from which they had come and the people passing there.

"No guilt?" he said in light mockery.

"None," she said, tossing her head in defiance of God knows whom.

"Shall we sit down? You can lecture me on whatever that window's all about."

"The passion of St. Vincent of Saragossa."

"The passion—a word with many meanings," he said, moving a chair to make more room between it and the next one.

"Let's not sit down," she said.

"I understand." Then: "Couldn't sit on these chairs anyway. They're built for midgets."

"There are not many men as tall as you in the countries where you find them."

"Or women as beautiful as you?"

"That is a *non sequitur*, Father Morrissey."

He nodded gravely. They moved beyond the altar-like table supporting a marble bas-relief. When they stood behind it, beneath the St. Vincent window, they could hold hands unobserved from outside the chapel. She squeezed his fiercely and then let go of it. A silence fell between them. She broke it presently to say, "Oh, Dan, what's to become of us?" She again laughed softly at herself, the hackneyed melodrama of her words.

"Before we're old and gray, priests will marry," he said.

"Divorced women?"

"Mmmmm. I have a way of forgetting about your husband."

"So do I when I'm with you."

From the chapel entry a guard spoke. "Step back, please."

Startled, they leapt apart.

"You are not allowed so close." The guard gestured them back to make clear his meaning. His accent was Hispanic.

"We are not touching anything," the priest said, speaking in Spanish. It was a language in which he was almost fluent. He was not recognizable as a priest; he wore a sports jacket and turtleneck sweater.

"It is my responsibility to say," the guard said aggressively, perhaps because he had been addressed in Spanish,

31

calling attention to his accent.

"Let's go, for heaven's sake," Kate said. "I want to see the modern glass."

The guard stood his ground while they walked past him, Kate holding high a very heavy head. "We've been drummed out of paradise." There was not much mirth in the laugh she managed.

"That guy's a bully," Morrissey said.

Kate had it on the tip of her tongue to say that bullies chose their prey carefully. She held her peace and once out of the Sculpture Court felt some restoration of her pride. She ought to have learned, living twenty years with Martin Knowles, how to ignore the tyranny of servants, public or personal. Instead, in a restaurant, for example, where Martin insisted that the service be impeccable, she sympathized with the underdog waiter, however truculently he came to heel. She glanced up at Morrissey. He winked at her and she almost took his hand to swing along with him in the carefree manner of young lovers.

At the heavy glass doors to the Garden Court an odd thing happened: as Kate pushed through, she caught the reflection of a man's face in the glass. His eyes were on hers, sad, questing eyes. She thought she recognized him, but as the glass receded with the door's opening, the image vanished, and when, having passed through, she looked back, there was no one in sight except Morrissey following close behind her.

"The strangest thing," she said. "I saw a face in the glass door, someone I thought I knew, but now it's gone."

"That was me," Morrissey said.

"No, I don't think so."

"Kate, shall we go on to your house and skip the art course?"

"It's too early," she said. "We need to give my house-keeper a little more time to get away."

Katherine and Martin Knowles had been active members of St. Ambrose parish since their marriage. Martin was a convert to Catholicism and, as Kate's mother said crankily at the wedding, it made him more Catholic than the pope. Indeed the Knowles, on their wedding trip to Italy, had knelt before Paul VI and kissed his ring. Kate wished at the time that it was John XXIII whose hand she touched. She could imagine that great hulk of a man with a heart to match, reaching down, taking her by both hands, and saying, "Come, you have as much right to the throne of Peter as I do." Not that she wanted to be pope any more than Betty Friedan did, but she had grown up in the early days of ecumenism and of Women's Liberation and was fiercely partisan. Martin took a dim view of both, and looked in recent years to John Paul II to put both church and women back on course.

Kate knew that the fabric of her faith was thinning before Daniel Morrissey crashed into her life. Martin's was of tougher stuff. Their son and daughter, in college, attended mass with some regularity, but made no secret of their differences with the church in matters they felt should be arbitrated directly between themselves and the Almighty. It was not something, however, they discussed with their father. Kate sometimes would have preferred not to be their confidante herself. She had been somewhat shaken on a recent Sunday when her daughter, visiting home, had gone to mass with her and, meeting Father Morrissey on the church steps afterwards, had declared of the dark-eyed, handsome priest, "What a waste!" On their way home, Kate silent, Sheila had teased her, "Did I shock you, Mother?"

"I agree!" Kate had said.

And Sheila: "Now I'm shocked."

On the day Kate and Morrissey met in the museum, they met again later that afternoon, but not by their own design. Twice a week Kate conducted what she loosely—very loosely—called an art class for youngsters attending St. Ambrose parochial school who, at the end of the school day, might otherwise have been unsupervised until a parent got home from work. St. Ambrose, once a wealthy Upper East Side parish, had become, like the neighborhood, a mix of the moderately rich and the borderline poor, the latter mostly Hispanic. The church had been undergoing extensive renovation at the time; the grime of sixty years was being removed from four large murals that depicted Christ's trial, death, resurrection and ascension. Much of the original paint came away with the dirt, however, and the restoration became more complicated and costly than the commissioned funds could cover. Martin Knowles made a substantial contribution to allow the work to go forward. Thus it was, Kate felt sure, that Monsignor Carey consulted with her on the work as it progressed. As soon as the restoration crew had closed up shop that day, the monsignor sent Morrissey to ask Mrs. Knowles, in the adjoining building, if she'd mind stepping over to the church for a few minutes. "You won't mind staying a while with the children, will you, Father?"

Morrissey did not mind. Seeing Kate, however briefly, eased the pain of separation that inevitably followed their hasty and furtive lovemaking. The way her eyes lit up when she saw him told of the same quick joy. They touched hands when she put the large scissors in his and told him he was journeyman to her apprentices. The color flared in her cheeks and she avoided looking at him. But very much on the alert was a youngster of eight or nine sitting across the table. His eyes, with the speed of arrows, darted from one adult's face to the other's.

Father Morrissey winked at him. He was a great winker, something that eased him out of many a confrontation. It was a mistake in this case. A little gleam of cunning shone in the boy's eyes. He had intuited something. "What's your name, young fellow?" the priest said.

"Rafael."

"Rafael," Morrissey repeated admiringly.

A pigtailed girl sitting next to the wily youngster said, "His name is José, father. Rafael is his brother's name."

"José is a fine name, too," Morrissey said, feeling like an idiot, making child's talk.

"She very nice woman," José said. "Smart."

"Who's that?"

"You know." The little demon rolled his eyes toward the door by which Kate had left them.

"Go back to work on whatever you were doing before I interrupted," the priest said.

"She say I'm going to be famous artist." The children were cutting out paper of different shapes and sizes and colors and pasting them together in such designs as they fancied or could manage. "Like Matisse." He said the name with practiced care.

The little girl giggled, "Mrs. Knowles calls all of us her little Matisses."

With lightning speed José grabbed a compass and tore it through the paste-up the little girl was working on. She howled, and Morrissey aimed a slap at the face of José— aimed it, but interrupted his own hand before it touched the boy. His dire intention became nothing more than a clap of noise. José did not even dodge what must have seemed to him an impending blow. The little girl reached over and snatched the collage José had been attempting and tore it apart. Very soon, up and down the long table, a dozen children were caught up in a frenzy of destruction. Those who reached for their neighbor's work too late to get it tore up their own, and shrieked with pleasure.

"Holy Mother of God," Morrissey murmured. "How do I handle this one?" Then, "Come on, you barbarians, let's get some exercise. On your feet and march!" He pushed one youngster in front of him and pulled one after him. He had to hunch down like Quasimodo. The only marching song he could think of was "Onward Christian Soldiers," and he belted out the tune in a sturdy baritone. The other kids fell in and soon they were marching around the room, strung together, hand in hand. Twice around and he called a halt and set them to cleaning up the mess.

José had joined the march, but now he sat, dark and sullen as a stone. When the little mischiefer next to him began to giggle and bite her lip, Morrissey realized something new was going on with José. He was probably peeing where he sat. If he was, his eyes never wavered from the priest's face while he did it.

"I always hesitate to ask you to come 'round and have a look, Mrs. Knowles," the monsignor said. "Ah, now, I'm supposed to call you Kate, Martin says, after all the years we've known each other, but I shy away from that as well. All the Protestants I know are on a first-name basis with their ministers and one another. I suppose it's all right, but I wouldn't want one of those little colts you're kind enough to corral after school, I wouldn't want one of them calling me Timothy to my face. I don't care what they call me behind my back. What was I saying?"

"I'm not sure," Kate said. She could no more call him Timothy than could Dan. Once in a while Dan spoke of him as the Old Man, but with reverence. Monsignor Carey had celebrated his fortieth year as a parish priest and he had trained his curates well. Two of them had been called to parishes of their own, and that, he had once told Martin, was as much as he could do for an ailing church. "It will come back to you," she said of whatever it was he'd been going to say.

"Things do," he said, "and some to haunt me." He squinted at her from under the shaggy black and white eyebrows. "You know, you don't look a day older than when I married you and Martin? He still calls you his bride, you know."

"I know," Kate said. She was sure there was nothing covert in his words, almost sure.

"He's a good man, Kate. There! I've called you Kate, and it didn't hurt a bit. Or did it you?"

"No, monsignor," she said, more stiffly than she'd intended.

He chortled. "I know when I've been put in my place. Well, as I was saying, I hope I'm not taking advantage of you, asking you to come and see the work in progress." They were standing beneath the scaffolding, before the mural of the crucifixion, the figures life-size. The garments and much of the background had been vividly repainted, so that the unfinished hands, feet and faces were pale and strangely ghost-like; the heads put her in mind of executioner's hoods. "You don't think the colors are too gaudy?" the old man ventured.

"Monsignor, shall I speak frankly?"

"Would I ask you otherwise?"

"You've put the restoration into the hands of a man the museum recommended. He's far more competent than I am." Kate was several notches above amateur status, but she was keenly aware that if it weren't for her husband's patronage, his financial influence, her standing in the art world wouldn't be much above that of a dilettante. Furthermore, she suspected the monsignor knew it as well as she did. He was courting favor with Martin. But to give him the benefit of the doubt, she said, "We've got to remember the restorer is working toward the original colors, not the faded pictures we've grown used to."

"You must be right. I only know what I like and I like what I'm used to. I'll get accustomed to this if I live long enough—and if I'm not shipped out."

"They wouldn't dare," Kate said.

"Wouldn't they now? Just watch in the next months. It will be me or Father Morrissey. I'll go to pasture, but they have their eye on him as a comer. And it's time. These young priests now—not that he's a youngster—but he goes along with the new generation: to them the priesthood is a profession, not a divine calling."

Kate murmured something. Her lips had gone dry. Her heart had gone dry. Not that she and Dan were unaware of the possibility of his being transferred. She sometimes thought Dan prayed for it, since he still prayed. Or so he said. Now and then they assured one another that they had no guilt, as though it were not bred in their bones. A parish of his own, what he had always wanted before his collision with her. Now it would be a kind of solution, however desperately she dreaded it. She waited while the monsignor stepped carefully over the drop sheets and turned off the floodlights.

"We'll go bankrupt keeping him in light," the monsignor said, returning to her side. "But I don't suppose Michelangelo was bargain basement either."

"I'd better get back and relieve Father Morrissey," Kate said.

"Did you ever meet Melodosi?" the monsignor asked,

staying the course of his own thoughts. "It's funny. I thought you knew him, too."

Kate waited for him to let her go, giving no sign of her impatience. The light of day had all but disappeared in the November twilight, the color of the stained glass high in the chancel window all but vanished. A stooped, shuffling, white-haired old man was silhouetted against the glow of many votive lights as he approached the statue of Virgin and child. He selected a taper and lit yet another candle among the glowing bank of them. The monsignor detained her, watching the petitioner. Kate could not remember having ever lighted a candle in church. It was a practice belonging to an earlier time than hers, or to a different class of people of whom, for some undefined reason, she felt envious at the moment.

The monsignor cleared his throat and a few seconds later a series of noisy clangs reverberated through the church as the petitioner dropped coins into the metal box.

The monsignor chortled quietly. "There'll be a few pesos in that lot," he whispered. Then: "Kneel down and I'll give you my blessing."

Kate went down on one knee and made the sign of the cross in unison with his.

The monsignor left her at the door to the passageway between church and school, and went on himself to the vestry and office, passing behind the main altar.

She felt choked, as though something in her chest was blocked. She sucked in the dead air of the passageway. It was such a little distance to the school door and yet the fire light above the door seemed remote. Two low-wattage bulbs caged in ceiling outlets scarcely lit a place already without shadows. No wonder it was called the tunnel. She wanted to hurry, to escape the echo of her own footfalls—if that was what she was hearing—but an inner warning held her back. The last few feet and she crashed into the brass bar that ought to have opened the door, but it did not budge. Again and again she pushed, but it was solidly in place, locked tight. She drew a deep breath and listened for the sound of the children: their room was not far from the door. But she did not hear a murmur. Could Dan have sent them home? And if he had, would he not have come this way himself and waited for her in the passage?

It came to her then that there had been a recent change in the lock-up system. Looters had come through the church and vandalized some of the classrooms. Now, at a given hour, you could pass from the school to the church, but not from the church to the school. Her panic eased and she turned back. She opened the church door to confront a figure palely lighted and seeming about to enter the passage she was leaving. He turned abruptly and went the way the monsignor had gone, passing behind the altar.

"Father?" she called after him. It might have been one of the other assistants. He did not return. She had only seen his face darkly, but she was sure it was the same she had seen reflected in the museum door that morning.

Morrissey was waiting for her, alone in the classroom she was allowed to use for her after-school art class. They both spoke at once, Kate asking where the children were, and Morrissey saying she'd been gone a long time.

"You look terrible," he said then. "What happened?"

Kate shook her head. "Nothing. I take it you dismissed the children?"

"They dismissed themselves, the little villains. I sent the one called José to the boy's room. He'd wet himself. And when he didn't come back, the youngster who sat next to him said he'd gone home. How she knew I don't know. I'm no good with children, Kate, and Monsignor Carey knows it. But every chance he gets, he throws me in with them."

"Daniel to the young lions," Kate said.

"It's no joke. That José or Rafael or whatever his name is a troublemaker."

"He's not," Kate said. "He's full of imagination and his home life is dreadful. He has an older brother he adores, but who beats up on him regularly."

Morrissey remembered how the youngster had not even flinched when he had come near hitting him. It crossed his mind that the boy wanted to be struck. "What did the monsignor have to say? I have to go in a minute."

"The troublemaker is the youngster who tattles on him all the time, Annabelle."

Morrissey was impatient. "Do you think the Old Man suspects us? That's the bottom line, isn't it?"

"No, I don't think he does. If he did, I think he'd come right out and ask what was going on between us."

"Just like that," Morrissey said, mocking her. "And what would you say to that?"

"Nothing, monsignor."

She could premeditate her lies, Morrissey thought. She was more honest than he was, who, at best, could figure out ways to evade the truth. "I must go," he said again. "I can go through the tunnel. You had to go around, didn't you?" She nodded. "Don't hang around here, Kate. These days you never know. Dear God, this place is depressing. No wonder kids grow up hating school."

"You'd better go, Dan. As you say, you never know." The only sound in the building was the pipes, the heat going on or off.

Neither of them had the impulse to embrace, to throw away caution, as was so often the case. As soon as the heavy

41

door to the passageway closed behind him, he wanted to go back and at least say he loved her as he had never hoped to love a woman. But the day so full of promise in the morning and its brief ecstasy in the afternoon had come to an end in a cold, bleak classroom under the merciless eyes of a too-curious child.

Kate slept with her husband that night. They had gone out to dinner with a client of Martin's. She had offered to make dinner, but Martin preferred a restaurant where, frankly, Kate could carry the principal burden of entertaining a man not easily entertained. She flirted with him openly, flatteringly, or as Martin put it, like a courtesan. It was intended as a compliment. There were not many things Martin liked better than to be the envy of his peers. She took a painful pleasure in making love with him when he was already so greatly pleased with her. She was great at giving pleasure, she thought ironically, and making do herself. The rites of married love had become mostly an agony. She had not reached the peak of self-deception where she could substitute one man for another in her fantasy. Afterwards, when Martin had returned to his own bed, contented and full of sleep, she was free to dream of Dan and a life with him.

Martin soon was breathing with deep regularity, while sleep was beyond her. She got up and went to the adjoining sitting room where, when Martin was away, she used to come up early in the night and read. The house had seemed too big. Now it was not big enough. At one of the deep, high windows with the shutters folded into the wall, she parted the drapes and stared out at the night.

There was no longer the street traffic after midnight in the East Nineties such as used to continue into the early hours of morning. An occasional taxi, a furtive pedestrian, drunk or

lost or homeless, with all his earthly goods stacked in a gro-
cery cart headed for a bench along the Central Park wall.
What would it be like to be in need, to be among the pitied or
among the despised, an object of surreptitious nudges? They
had been cast out of paradise, she remembered jesting to Dan
in the museum. But suppose they were discovered? They
must not let that happen. If there was to be a future for them,
they must themselves take the first step at bringing it about.
They must salvage some small dignity at least. Theirs was not
the first such love in history, only the first for them. The children would understand, Sheila certainly, in time. And
Martin: she could name a half-dozen women who would
open their arms to him. His hurt would pass, perhaps even his
outrage. Dan could make a good confession and petition the
archdiocese, the Vatican if necessary, to be released from his
vows. They had spoken of it: such release could only happen
after a period of separation from her and from the most
sacred of his duties. It would not happen, she knew that. Dan
would rather wait and pray for the day that priests could
marry, so self-persuaded the day was coming he could grant
himself premature indulgence. And to tell the truth and
shame the devil, she too preferred to wait. Be honest, Kate:
now is forever.

Her thoughts became as a thousand tongues babbling
half-finished sentences from her subconscious. Try as she
might, she could not hold those flashes of memory she
wanted most to dwell on now—their first touch, love first
spoken, promises, longings shared, such as for the sweet
peace they had never known of sleep together after love. She
stared at the street lamp beneath her window, to hold onto
that longing at least. But it became a halo, then a face: it
might have been the image of St. Francis as on the prayer card
that memorialized her mother's death. She could not hold to

that either: it had become the face as she had glimpsed it in the museum door, the face confronting her at the tunnel door. The pounding in her ears had to be her own heartbeat and not the rhythm of running footsteps. When she closed her eyes, opened them, and looked again, there was only the street lamp and its misty halo.

At dawn, Martin, an early riser, found her curled up in an afghan, deep in a sedated sleep on the divan.

Most Sundays Father Morrissey said the Spanish language mass at twelve-thirty. The monsignor insisted. He was very proud of him, his non-Hispanic assistant pastor who had learned the language of the growing majority of their congregation. When Morrissey pulled a blooper during his homily, the Old Man said of the barely suppressed giggles, "Never mind. It keeps them alert waiting to catch you up." These Sundays Morrissey had more to overcome than his mistakes in Spanish grammar. He had no choice, he told himself, but to say mass: the people expected it of him, and too, a priest, once ordained, never lost the power of his priesthood, no matter into what delinquency he strayed. He could be forbidden to use the power, but he could not be deprived of it, and the bread and wine he consecrated in the Lord's name became the living presence as truly as if St. Peter himself stood at the altar.

Robed in the purple of Advent, he waited at the back of the church with the new priest and the readers and servers taking their places for the processional. In the sanctuary, the musicians were tuning up, the choir arranging chairs to their liking. He watched the latecomers scrambling for seats. The youngster José came with his mother. If the boy had not looked around at the assembling processional, Morrissey might have happily missed him. His mother dragged him forward and then pushed him ahead of her into a pew. While she covered her face in prayer, he turned and stared back blatantly at the priest.

To Morrissey's dismay, Kate entered the church. She was alone. He had never seen her at this mass before. She generally attended the eight o'clock with Martin or the ten-thirty if she came on her own. If she saw him, she gave no sign. She sat near the back, but close enough to José for him to see and recognize her. Surreptitiously, his hand half-hidden by his shoulder, he waved at her. The little demon had a crush on her. Whether or not Kate saw him, the priest couldn't tell. She gave no sign of it. He tried then to convince himself that José might well be waving to someone else. Everybody knew everybody in their community, and the latecomers were still scrambling into the church, dodging the barricades set up to protect the restoration riggings. The monsignor himself was routing traffic.

The musicians struck up, the *pandereta, the maraca,* the guitars, and the fervent, harsh voices of the choir. As the monsignor had said to him once: if they couldn't beguile you into heaven with their singing, they could scare you half the way. The congregation rose and sang with the choir as the procession got under way, white-robed servers, girls and boys, readers, the new associate just up from Puerto Rico, and the censor-swinging acolyte, laying down a smoke screen before him.

Morrissey sat, three-quarter face to the congregation, the young associate at his side. There was so little for the celebrant to do in the contemporary mass, so much of the ritual given up to the lay participants, with a solacing share to the women. Clouded with incense before reading the gospel, he lost his concentration. *There would be signs in the sun and the moon and the stars . . . the roaring of the sea, men fainting for fear and for expectation . . . they will see the son of man coming upon a cloud with great power and majesty. . . .* He stumbled over the Spanish word, and the new priest whispered it, the loudspeaker picking up his voice as he had not intended.

With the offertory of the mass finally upon him and with effort beyond what he had been equal to until that moment, he said the words of the consecration—This is my body . . . this is my blood—words he knew the Lord himself would keep pure.

As far as he could see, Kate was not among those who thronged to the sanctuary steps to receive communion. He would not have expected her to, but suddenly before him was José, his small hands fisted at his side when the priest offered him the wafer, his lips, too, tightly closed against it. The boy's mother prodded and scolded him from behind. He had come to the table but he would not partake. His eyes were coals of defiance. Father Morrissey moved to the nearest server and changed places with him. There was only a small disruption until José's mother grabbed her son's arm and flung him away, crying out, "Perdido! Perdido!" Lost: it had the ring of a flamenco lament, and it carried through the church. José spat in the direction of the altar and ran from the steps.

Kate could not see what had happened at the altar steps, but those who had seen it were calling out condemnation after the fleeing youngster. She would have been willing to swear that José Mercado was not a bad boy. Troubled, yes, and obviously now in trouble. She left the church, trying to draw as little attention as possible. She was well known as Martin's wife and for her own outreach as well. She squeezed the numerous hands extended to her, and made it to the vestibule before the mass was finished. She ought not to have come to this mass. Besides her own unease, it was not fair to Dan, and encountering the monsignor on the church steps, she tried to think of an excuse for being there at that hour.

The monsignor had something else on his mind. "Did you notice the youngster flying out of the church? I tried to lay hold of him. Slippery as an eel. Do you know what he did? He spat out the sacrament. They're not being well taught, you know. That one should never have made his first communion."

Kate, not about to debate the boy's demeanor with the monsignor, gave a nod to indicate concern and escaped. Someone was following her. She knew an instant of fear before she realized it was José. She waited for him and they walked in silence for almost another block before Kate finally said, "Do you want to tell me what's the matter?"

José shook his head and they walked on. He was wearing a fake leather jacket, frayed at the cuffs and at least two sizes too big for him; the T-shirt underneath was thin, the red apple on its front badly faded. His jeans were clean and his sneakers had been new at the start of the school year. His dark hair rose and fell as the wind tossed through it.

"Aren't you cold?" Kate asked. She was wishing herself that she had worn a sweater beneath her coat.

Again he shook his head. He wiped his nose on the back of his hand. They walked on.

They had almost reached Kate's building. She wondered if it was wise to let him know where she lived, and then decided, wise or not, it showed some respect for his fiery young person. Once in class she had boosted his ego by calling him a young Matisse and showing him pictures of the artist's windows. He took everything he did in class home with him after that. Or said he did. He liked to please her. He spoke English as well as any of the children. His mother spoke Spanish. His older brother spoke both languages, but beat José if he did not speak English. José loved him, anyway.

Reaching the entryway to the townhouse where she and Martin lived, she told the boy that this was where she must leave him and proposed to shake his hand. "Where do you live, José?"

He jerked his head toward the north, and ignored the hand she offered him so that Kate quickly withdrew it. "You should go home now and not catch cold," she said.

"Why you don't go to communion this morning?" he blurted out, the first words he had spoken to her all the way home.

Kate was stunned. When she was his age, the lie would have been so simple: I broke my fast. That didn't matter any more. Now all she could do was fall back on authority. "You don't ask questions like that of older people, José. Go home now." As though he were a stray dog. When she turned from him, she saw Martin watching from the window of his study. She waved. He nodded appreciatively, as though he took for granted she would be accompanied by a child or children. When she looked back from the vestibule, José had disappeared.

"I saw it with my own eyes," the monsignor said, waiting in the vestry with Morrissey while he disrobed.

Morrissey removed the stole, touched it to his lips and laid it away in the drawer. "I'm sorry, monsignor, but the boy didn't receive communion at all. From what I could tell, his mother was insisting that he do, and he was determined not to."

The monsignor grunted. "Everybody wanted to stone him, as though the mass wasn't half-circus already. Mind, I'm not criticizing the new liturgy." He waited until

Morrissey had pulled the amice over his head. "Was it you or the Almighty he was boycotting, do you think?"

The wily old fox, Morrissey thought. "It might have been me. We had an altercation of sorts when you sent me to sit in for Mrs. Knowles the other day."

The monsignor took longer to respond than Morrissey could handle, uneasy as he was at having even mentioned Kate's name. "I've never been very good with the children, as you know."

"Were you never a child yourself, Dan?"

The use of his name eased Morrissey's discomfort. "I spent most of my youth in fear of my father."

"So you've said. A strapping fellow like you?"

" 'Mark my words, laddy,' he'd say, 'I'll bring you down to my size one of these days.' And God knows, he tried."

The monsignor shook his head. "Well, I'm glad it's you the youngster's mad at and not the Lord. He'll get over it without damaging his faith. But they do hold a grudge, don't they?" he added, presumably of the Hispanic people.

Morrissey was holding a grudge himself against the youngster who, he felt, had deliberately intended to humiliate him. He had brought hate to the altar with him. It shone from his eyes. If he had said it aloud, it could not have been more clear. The priest could be grateful for one thing: if he had not been holding the sacrament in his hands, he'd have been hard put not to shake the boy till his teeth rattled. Even now it was hard for him to thank the Lord for getting in the way. But the monsignor left him, and before he went out of the church himself, he stepped into the sanctuary and said a prayer of contrition.

That afternoon he walked over to the Jesuit parish a few blocks from St. Ambrose. It had been some time since he had gone to confession. Sitting with his confessor, he named as the offense for which he was most deeply sorry his intense dislike for a child in the parish school. The Jesuit wanted to know if he had ever touched the boy. Morrissey told how close he had come to striking him.

"That's not what I had in mind," the other priest said.

"No," Morrissey said, "it's not like that." He completed his confession without ever mentioning adultery or the breaking of his vow of celibacy.

Kate next met with the children the following Tuesday. She had put in for a bus to transport them now that the days were getting short. It would not be available until later in the week, so she decided to drive them home in her own car since she expected to use it later. Meanwhile, she chided them gently: they ought not to go off on their own as had happened on Friday.

"The padre say 'Get out!' " José said.

"I don't think that's so, is it?" She looked from one child to the next.

A lot of little heads nodded that it was. Annabelle volunteered to explain. "José tore up my picture and Father Morrissey slapped him."

"Right here," José said, pointing to his cheek. "I tell my brother, and he say, 'Next time you tell me, and I take care the *gringo* priest.' "

"He makes us all stand up and march around the room," someone else volunteered.

"He say I don't have to go to boys' room. He makes me piss on floor," José added.

"That's enough," Kate said. If she had been told at the moment that the children were possessed by demons, she'd have believed it. Or was it Dan of whom they'd taken possession? Something had happened in her ten- or fifteen-minute absence that day that had thrown them into chaos. She set them to making mobiles, having brought a model from her studio at home.

When she was helping José, she saw that he was looking at her, not at the supposed-to-be mobile. "The priest come today?" he asked finally.

"Not that I'm expecting, José. But then I didn't expect him on Friday either. The monsignor sent him."

"How come?"

"Because the monsignor wanted to see me. Now pay attention or you won't be able to do this by yourself."

José had one more question: "Why you teach us like this?"

"Now let me ask a question, José Mercado: Why are you asking me all these questions?"

He turned his sweetest smile on her. The shyness of it had always beguiled her. "I like you," he said.

She was less than beguiled at the moment. More cunning than beguilement, she thought, and that was distressing. To what purpose? The phrase, *the gringo priest,* stayed with her. "If you really like me, you will make me a perfect mobile."

And with the use of teeth and tongue as well as fingers, he made one that almost hung in balance.

Kate could not make up her mind whether or not to mention Morrissey's misadventure with the children to him. The variation in their stories and his was troublesome. She did not like to ask him outright if he had struck the boy, even though she could not believe that he had done it.

After delivering the children that afternoon she drove around until she found a parking place on the street some distance east. She told Morrissey where the car was when he phoned. They planned to meet there after he had said the rosary at a wake a few blocks away. Martin was in Washington preparing for an early morning meeting. He was not due home until the next evening, but meetings could be canceled and the anxiety of having Morrissey in the house at night was too much. The phantom face, as it sometimes did now, reappeared in her mind's eye after she had given a few minutes' thought to the possible emergency measures if Martin should return to find Dan there. She could pretend, for example, sudden illness so that she had wanted a priest and phoned the rectory. Again she heard her own heartbeat and thought of pounding feet. She tried to stare through the image. It was too bright, featureless, but it would not go away. She finally escaped it by going into Martin's study and re-reading a letter from her son that she had left on her husband's desk. Her forehead was moist. If she could not control her own imagination, what chance had she of carrying off an emergency deception?

Morrissey lingered at the wake longer than he would have chosen to, but the family were longtime members of St. Ambrose, among the few, like the Knowleses, who were generations deep in the neighborhood. He knew his popularity among them. More than once he had been told that he was one of theirs. Their generosity and participation in causes he championed recommended him to certain archdiocesan committees and to the occasional chaplainship. Striding along the streets to where Kate was waiting for him, he thought of the jeopardy in which their affair was placing him, and put it out of mind instantly. Once. Once in his life, he told himself, he would know sexual joy, and be the better priest for its denial ever after.

The car was warm when he climbed in alongside her. Their embrace was long and deep. "Oh, my God," he said, after a moment. "I needed that." Then: "Where can we go?"

"I know a place," Kate said.

She drove down and across town to the waterfront in the

Twenties, where a few cars were parked, well-spaced apart.

"Isn't this where the gays hang out?" he asked.

"Yes."

He shuddered within his topcoat as he thought about what was going on in those other cars. "Let's get the hell out of here."

"Any suggestions?" Kate asked when they had driven in and around the Village in silence for a few minutes. She parked in front of a fire hydrant.

"Isn't Martin in Washington?"

"He's supposed to be," she said.

"In other words, you'd rather risk us getting caught in a police raid on Sodom."

"It is tacky, isn't it?" Kate said in bitter sarcasm.

Things went from bad to worse as time ran ahead of them and frustration mounted. Morrissey accused her of flirting with the monsignor, something he had only vaguely thought about until now, as her way of diverting the old man from their interest in one another. It opened the opportunity for Kate to ask him just what had happened with the children the previous Friday. "*Did* you strike José?"

"He's a dirty little liar if he says I did. Believe me, I wanted to, and he had it coming, but I caught myself in time. He's a troublemaker, Kate, and you'll be sorry if you coddle him. He's got ideas about us right now—the way some kids his age catch on to people when their prurient little minds are waking up."

"Prurient," Kate repeated.

"You know what I mean."

"Yes, Dan. I think I do. Now tell me what happened in church on Sunday."

"You should know better than to come to that mass, Kate."

"What happened?" she repeated.

"He refused to take communion from me. Made fists of his hands. His mouth was a steel trap. Kate, these Hispanic kids are so far ahead of us in sexual awareness, you've got to be careful with them."

"I will," she said.

But Morrissey was sure she'd take the youngster's side against him. It was incredible that one little black-eyed peasant could destroy something as beautiful as what he and Kate had between them. In no way would he let it happen. He laid his hand on hers. "Kate, could you teach me how to love children the way you've taught me how to love?"

José turned up at art class on Friday showing signs of either having been in a fight or having been abused. The visible marks were a purpling bruise on his cheek and a cut in his lip that bled in his one attempt to smile. Kate's inclination was to put an arm around him. She thought of Morrissey's counsel not to coddle him, but that was not what restrained her. There was a watchfulness about the boy, and she felt that to show concern might put him to flight. The other children shied away from him. They gave him more work room at the table than he needed. In fact, he didn't need work room at all. He simply sat there and did nothing except pluck at the edges of his drawing book with dirty fingernails, as though he could not wait for the class to end.

That afternoon saw the first run of the minibus Kate had arranged for. She shepherded the youngsters onto it herself, a noisy lot, and only at the last minute discovered that José was not among them. It was Annabelle who gave her the clue as to where he might be. Kate sent the bus on and went back into the school building. Sure enough, beneath a closed toilet door in the boys' room, a pair of nearly new sneakers were to be seen.

"José, it's Mrs. Knowles. The others have gone. I'll take you home myself if you like."

Silence.

"José?"

"No."

"No what?"

"No, *gracias*."

"They'll close up the building soon. The custodian will make you leave."

He came out then. "I not go home," he said.

"Let's talk about it," Kate said.

They went back to the classroom and Kate turned on the lights she had extinguished when they'd left. Dan was right. It was a dreary place, especially without the children. Kate sat on the table, positioning herself between him and the door. The boy stood, his hands folded over his fly.

"Is it your brother?" Kate asked gently.

"What you know?" His eyes challenged her.

"I know he hurts you badly sometimes."

She decided that was not what he had feared she might know. She waited.

"You no tell the *padre?*" he said finally.

"Why would I tell him?"

"Because . . . because, you know."

Kate did not follow up. She was remembering his one question Sunday: *Why you not go to communion?* "What did happen to you, José?"

His eyes grew large and round as he began to tell her. "The big old building near my house? The doors . . . boom, boom, boom, boom . . ." He gestured a row of doors such as sometimes line the street where a building is being demolished. "The windows broke."

Kate nodded. She could visualize the building and knew

its approximate location. A new housing project was about to get under way on that whole block.

"My brother, I see him meet his girl, so I no get on the school bus. I follow them. I no come to school today. They go in this building. I go in and listen. Where they go? Then I hear them. I know what they doing. *Si?*"

"Go on," Kate said.

"Then she scream. Terrible, and Raffie swear. He call her bad names. She no scream no more, and pretty soon I hear Raffie come running. I hide so he don't see me, but he no look. He run out. So I run out too. Across the street he look back and see me. When he catches me, he hit me. He say I get hit worse if I tell. I promise to no tell, but he hit me more." José pointed to his lip. "First I go home and hide in basement. Then I go upstairs. Raffie no there. I watch TV till I come here."

"José, do you know the girl?"

"She Rafael's girlfriend."

"Do you know her name?"

He shook his head, but Kate suspected that he did.

Whether it was the right moment or the wrong one, it was the moment at which Morrissey appeared in the doorway. She put one last question to the boy before acknowledging the priest's presence. "Have you seen the girl since?"

José did not answer. He was staring at the priest defiantly.

Kate looked 'round. "Good afternoon, Father."

Morrissey, who had approached the room without making a sound, had been listening outside the door. Without responding to Kate's greeting, he said, "Don't you think we should go and see if she's still there, José?"

"I no want to go there, Father."

"But suppose the police say you have to go?" The priest

took a few tentative steps into the room.

"I don't know where. I forget," José said.

Morrissey repeated Kate's question: "Did you ever see the girl again?"

José made a break for the door. Kate almost intercepted him, but Morrissey caught her arm and held her until the boy was gone.

"You have no right to interfere," Kate said. "This is my place."

"So we're talking about rights now. I didn't know they went with a relationship like ours. Kate, that boy was lying to you. He's got you in the palm of his hand and he knows it. You must not get us involved."

"I had no intention of getting us involved."

"You don't know what he'll say he saw or who he'll say it to. Suppose he says he's seen us together in some compromising place or situation?"

"But he hasn't, and who would believe him?"

"You'd be surprised. I didn't strike him, but that's his story, and I think you, for one, bought it."

Kate thought of José's brother; what he'd do to "the *gringo* priest." He had been told something certainly.

"He's a good liar, Kate."

"A better one than you or me? And is that what's important now? We should forget the girl. Is that it? Even if she's lying half-dead in some wreck of a building?"

"Frankly, I don't think there is a girl."

"Do you care?"

"If I thought there was a girl, yes. Then I'd say we should find a telephone right now and call the police."

Kate thought about it. "Do you think that's what he wanted me to do?"

"Oh, no." Morrissey gave a small, dry laugh. "It's what

he's afraid I'll do. Kate, ask yourself: Why did he come to you with this story?"

"You tell me," she said.

Morrissey thought for a long moment about what he would say. "I'll give it a shot," he said. "He's made up a story—a street story, common as dirt, as close as he could come to telling you what's in his mind."

"About us?" Kate said, incredulous.

"You asked me to tell you, and now you'll listen to the whole thing. I can't say what triggered his imagination, but he knew from the moment he saw our hands touch when I took the scissors from you that there was something going on between us." Morrissey threw up his hands. "Maybe he's warning you—danger ahead! I don't know."

"Don't be angry, Dan."

"I'm not angry. I'm ashamed, if you want to know."

Ashamed, Kate thought, another word for guilt.

"I was a child just like him," Morrissey went on. "In adolescence I grew in prurience. My father tried to beat it out of me. Instead he beat it in. I fled to the priesthood. I thought it was my penance. It was my salvation."

Kate slipped down from the table and offered her hands, caution be damned. He shook his head, smiled a little and left her. She heard the click of the tunnel door.

She sat again for a few minutes, thinking.

Had their affair been inevitable, a kind of Satanic justice to be satisfied after all these years? And if it was over, was he free now of the demon guilt forever? It was not in the nature of man. Or woman. She thought of the phantom face that had seemed to pursue her, to accuse her. No. That was not its mission. It followed, sometimes with a rhythmic beat, like the Hound of Heaven.

She left the school and went into the church by the side

door, the only one left open at that hour of the day. The high-intensity lights were focused on the Crucifixion mural, the artist himself straddling a plank in the scaffolding as he worked overtime. He was almost finished. With the Lord's face and one of the women's restored, Melodosi was studying his work on the other Mary. Even before he looked down at her, Kate knew his half-familiar face to be that of the phantom she had chosen to pursue her.

She moved on to a pew in a darkened place. It had been a long time since she had prayed with her heart and mind, and on her knees. A simple prayer: *Lord, I need help.* She left the church determined to go to the police with José's story, but when she reached the street, she saw two nuns waiting to be admitted at the St. Ambrose convent door. She got to them in time to enter the building with them, and very shortly Sister Josephine Reilly came to her in the parlor. As soon as the nun saw who it was, she said, "I know, it's about José Mercado again."

"I just have a question," Kate said. "Was he absent from school this morning?"

"No," the young nun said. "As soon as I saw him in first class, I sent him to the infirmary, but bad luck that it was, the nurse was out today. I cleaned him up a bit myself between classes."

"Did he tell you what happened to him?"

The nun gave a great rolling shrug. "I think he said his brother beat him up—was it for talking back to their mother? Who knows with José?"

Who knows indeed, Kate thought.

A week passed before she heard from Morrissey. He called to say he was going upstate to the Trappist monastery on retreat. "Kate . . ." She could hear the deep intake of breath.

"You don't need to say anything, Dan."

"I'm grateful to you for understanding."

"And I to you, Father Morrissey."

The Puppet

Over the ring of the doorbell came the cry, "Help me, Julie . . .
Let me in!"

Julie, out of bed before she was rightly awake, pulled on
her robe and ran, barefoot, to the front of the shop. It was
half-past one in the morning. She unbolted the door and
opened it on the latch. Her upstairs neighbor, Rose Rodriguez, was shivering in a silvery dress that glowed in the stark
Manhattan street light. Julie let her in, then bolted the door
and lighted a lamp.

"I don't know where Juanita is. She's not in her bed. I
thought maybe she comes to you?"

Julie shook her head. "Sit down while I get my slippers."

The chair creaked with its burden. In the years Julie Hayes
had occupied the shop, the ground floor apartment on West
44th Street, Mrs. Rodriguez had put on weight. Her one
child, Juanita, had grown from a string bean to puberty with a
sudden promising beauty.

Mrs. Rodriguez pointed at the row of dolls when Julie returned. They sat on a table, their backs against the wall.
"They are Juanita's, no?"

"We've been mending them," Julie said. "Now tell me
what's with Juanita?"

"It's boys. I know it's boys."

You ought to know, Julie thought. It was apparent Mrs. Rodriguez had just returned from an evening out. Her husband
wouldn't know about it. Juanita would. Julie was not a great
hater, but she would have been hard put to find a kind word

for the woman now twisting off the flashy rings from her fingers. "Where do you think she is? Let's start with that."

"She wants to go to her friend Elena's for supper. I say okay, but you be home by nine o'clock. The whole holiday weekend and she hasn't done her homework."

"*Did* she come home?"

"Julie . . ." The woman's face became a mask of contrition. "She has a very good father but not so good mother. You know?"

Julie ignored the ploy for sympathy. "Isn't it possible she tried to call you? To ask if she could stay overnight? And then stayed anyway when she couldn't reach you?"

"She knows better. Papa will not give permission. He will kill me. . . ." The woman began to sob.

"Stop that!" Julie shouted. "Let's call her friend's house right now."

"You know her number, Julie?"

"Don't you?"

"I don't even know her name except Elena."

"Then you can't do anything till morning. I can call the police. . . ."

"No. No police. They come and ask questions."

"Yeah."

Mrs. Rodriguez brushed away green tears. Her mascara was running. "You are right. She stays with Elena, I think. That's what I tell Papa if he looks and sees she's not in her bed. A wild man."

"First thing in the morning, call the school. Ask for the principal. Whoever you get, find out Elena's last name, her phone number. . . ."

The woman laid her hand on Julie's. "Please, will you call? Say it's for me, Señora Rodriguez. Say I don't speak very good English. That's the truth, no?"

"Mrs. Rodriguez . . ."

"Please, you call me Rose. We are friends, no?"

Julie could not go back to sleep. She listened for Juanita's father to come home from work, a tired, bemused man who moonlighted on a second job while his wife moonlighted in her fashion. Juanita had grown up a silent, angry child who beat her dolls and pulled off their arms and legs. Now she and Julie were putting them together again with glue and heavy thread, a Christmas project for the really poor. It had taken Julie a long time to make her smile, then laugh, to make her see the dolls as little Juanitas. A lot of her own angry childhood had gone into the making.

Mr. Rodriguez came home. Julie waited for the explosion, the reverberations of which would run through the building. But none came. The woman would have persuaded him the child was asleep in her bed. Julie sat up and phoned the local precinct. The only complaints involving children were drug-related: downtown bookings, parents contacted.

"How about the prostitutes—any young ones?" The wildest possibility.

"They're all young—and as old as Magdalene," the desk sergeant said. Then: "This wasn't a sweep night, Julie."

Nothing came of inquiries to the local hospitals.

Julie lay back and thought about when she had last seen the youngster. Late afternoon yesterday. Probably when she was coming home to ask permission to go to Elena's. What was she wearing besides the red, white, and green streamers? Julie couldn't remember. The Italian colors were for the Columbus Day Street Fair. Nor could she remember Juanita's ever mentioning Elena. She was only beginning to make friends. So, thank God for Elena. Sleep finally came.

★ ★ ★ ★ ★

The girl opened her eyes. She seemed to be dreaming of waking up, but she had to be still asleep. She was lying in a huge, strange bed under a blanket with her clothes on. The room was dark except for a patch of gray light in the ceiling. Curled up on her side, her thumb in her mouth, she stared at the light. It looked more like a sheet floating up there, but the flickering lights of a plane appeared and moved quickly out of sight again. She heard the roar go away. It was a skylight in the ceiling, something she had seen only in a movie.

She tried to wake up. She bit her thumb, and when it hurt she knew that she was already awake. Then she remembered what had happened to her before the sleep: the woman and a man in the dirty lobby of an old theater where she had gone to see the puppets. At the fair the woman had told her about them and promised to show her how they worked. She had wanted to learn how to make puppets and how to make them act. The woman said she was a natural. She and Julie might even use the dolls and make their own puppet show. But there weren't any puppets, and she knew the minute the door had closed behind her that she should never, never have gone there. The woman grabbed her and covered her mouth when she started to scream; the man held her legs and roped them together, then knocked them out from under her, sat on her, pinned her arm down, and must have stuck a needle in her. The place in the hollow of her arm hurt now when she touched it. She distinctly heard him say, "Five minutes." She tried to scratch and bite. The man swore at her and the woman said, "For Christ's sake, Danny, do you want her looking like a battered child?" Her memory stopped right there. Now the important thing was she had to go to the bathroom.

She inched her way to the edge of the bed in the direction she was facing. Something white stood on the floor a few feet from the bed—a bucket, she made out after a few seconds of study. She would have to use it, and maybe that was what it was there for. She crawled to it. It seemed safer to stay close to the floor. She wondered if her shoes were in the bed but didn't think so. She squatted over the bucket but nothing happened. While she waited she made out the shapes of some scary figures on the other side of the bed—a lot of chalky white people just standing. They seemed to be moving toward her. She tried to cry out, but couldn't, and her legs were shaking. She was sure she was going to fall. She managed not to, and the figures didn't come round the bed. They weren't even moving. Statues? If that was what they were, could one of them be the Blessed Virgin? "Hail Mary, full of grace, the Lord is with thee. . . ." She heard her own voice mumbling the prayer, then the beginning trickle of her water, then the gush, noisy in the pail.

She had just finished when the door opened behind her and sent a splash of light across the room. The man came in and lit a lamp on a table near the door.

"Figured out what that was for, did you? You're a smart girl."

She made no sound or move.

"Get back into bed and stay there till she brings your breakfast. I don't want you messing round the studio. Do you know what a studio is? It's where artists work."

If she ran for the door, what would happen? He was too close to it and she couldn't run. She couldn't even move. Only her heart bumped inside her.

"Did you hear me? Into bed!"

"No."

He grinned at her and took the hypodermic needle from his pocket.

She lunged, stumbling, toward the bed.

The guidance counselor, Dr. Alverez, sent Elena Cruz back to her classroom. Julie used the counselor's phone to call Mrs. Rodriguez and tell her the news was not good. "You'd better waken your husband and then call the police, nine one one. Juanita did not go to Elena's house at all last night. Elena was at her aunt's house for dinner. In other words, Juanita has been missing since you last saw her. You simply must call the police."

"Julie, please!" The woman's voice rose hysterically.

"I'll call you later," Julie said and hung up.

The counselor was watching Julie with an appraising eye. "You know, don't you, you're the best thing that ever happened to Juanita."

"Doesn't help much now, does it?"

"If there's anyone she'll get in touch with it's you."

"So if I don't hear from her, where is she? What's the worst possibility you can think of, doctor?"

The counselor gave an enormous sigh. "That she was abducted. But if she was, she must have set herself up for it willingly—the lie about dinner at Elena's."

"Her mother thinks it's all about boys," Julie said.

"I wish it were. Ridiculous of me to say that, but the boys are a lot more interested in Juanita than she is in the boys."

"Do you know what her home situation is like?"

Alverez nodded. "Her father works long hours. Whatever her mother does while he's away, Juanita's ashamed of it."

"She usually stops at my place on the way home if I'm there. Yesterday she didn't. I just happened to see her go by. I think she'd been to the street fair. If you'd ask her classmates whether anyone saw her—where and what time—it would be great. When I went out not long after I saw her, I found a flyer stuck in my mail drop. Now I wonder if she put it there.

Maybe. You try to think of everything. This was about a rally of the West Side women to close up the porn shops in the neighborhood."

Alverez smiled. "Well, I can tell you this: If there's a budding feminist in the sixth grade, it's Juanita Rodriguez."

"Take a bite, honey, or I'll eat it. Didn't your mother ever say, 'If you don't eat it, I will'?"

Juanita did not answer. She was sitting at the table, the big woman between her and the door. It was daylight, but the room was lighted mostly by long tubes in the ceiling. There weren't any windows except the one in the roof. The man, Danny, was poking around among the statues and moving some boxes. There were paintings, too, one on a three-legged stand and others stacked on their sides. Danny wasn't doing anything, only moving things around. With his little eyes and skinny moustache he didn't look to her like an artist.

The woman broke off a piece of the Danish, touched Juanita's tight lips with it, and then ate it herself. Her fingernails were like dabs of blood, her mouth a red smear. Even her hair was red. She was as old as Mama, a lot older than Julie. Everybody would be looking for her, but where would they look? Papa would shout and whack her mother. Then he'd cry.

"Take some coffee, Juanita. It won't hurt you, I promise."

"You promised there were puppets." Her first words except for the "No" to the needle.

"We do make puppets."

The man gave a bark of laughter.

"Shut up, Danny. And you're not supposed to touch any of their things back there. It's in the agreement."

"Fuck the agreement."

67

"Don't you talk like that in front of her," the woman shouted.

"What in hell is going on with you, Dee?"

"Why don't you go out and look for what you're supposed to be looking for?"

"Because it's nine A.M. and nothing's open yet." He came out from among the statues and stopped at the table. "The lights in here are no damn good for us. We should've known that."

"Then get some that are! Honest to God, Danny, you're in New York City."

"Don't hassle me, Dee. You're the one jumped the gun, though I'm damned if I see why. Little Miss Perfect here." He caught a handful of Juanita's hair and pulled her head back—not roughly, but not gently either. He looked at her from her eyes to as far down as he could see and then let go. He poked his finger at the woman's face. "Just don't get too fond of her. She's a puppet, remember."

Julie, after several phone calls, reached an organizer of the antiporn rally. She promised an item in the *Our Beat* column and then told of the missing youngster. "It's a long shot, but if you were handing out flyers at the street fair yesterday, I wonder if you saw her."

"I wasn't there myself, but there was an incident at the fair that might have involved your young person. Let me give you the number of Sue Laughlin. You mustn't take her literally if she makes it sound like gang rape. That's just Sue."

A chorus of infant and toddler voices rang through Julie's conversation with Sue Laughlin. "I thought the girl was older—sixteen, maybe. And she did volunteer. Anyway—shut up, Jamie. Can't you see Mommy's on the phone?—anyway, she was handing out our flyers when this gang of young jocks started to tease her—'What's pornography, Juanita?' That sort of thing."

"Did they call her by name? It's important."

"How would I know her name if they hadn't? Then one of them snatched the flyers from her and they all clowned around throwing them into the air. And what did she do? She grabbed an umbrella from a concession stand and began thrashing the mischief out of them."

Gang rape, Julie thought.

"They ran off and the guy selling the umbrellas tried to make her buy the one she'd taken. I was going to say something, but a woman who'd been watching the whole thing said she'd buy the umbrella."

"Did you know the woman?"

"No. I don't think she's from the neighborhood. There were hundreds of people, you know."

Julie felt herself tighten up. "Did she speak to Juanita?"

"I couldn't say for sure. I just wasn't paying attention after that."

"Could you describe the woman?"

"A big, solid woman, well dressed but flashy, too much makeup, red hair . . ."

Julie reached Detective Russo at precinct headquarters with her bits of information. Dominic Russo and she were old friends so he could say frankly that he would give it what time he could, but from her parents' report the youngster sounded like a runaway. The case would go to Missing Persons within twenty-four hours. "We'll give out her description at roll call and put it on the bulletin board. But you know how many kids hit the streets every day."

"Yeah."

"Most of them come home in a day or two."

"Some don't ever. I'll keep in touch, Dom."

"Don't I know that," he said.

Julie went upstairs to see the Rodriguezes as soon as they got home. Juanita's father was sitting in the kitchen, his head in his hands. He looked up at her when she laid her hand on his shoulder. His eyes were wet. "Why she do this to us? Why?"

Julie, to reassure them of the girl's resourcefulness, told them how Juanita had confronted the boys who were taunting her. Mrs. Rodriguez turned and stormed at her husband, "Men are pigs. You're all pigs!" It ought to have been funny, Julie thought, but it wasn't.

Juanita sat on the bathroom stool in a silk robe that was much too big for her. She had taken a shower she hadn't wanted and washed her hair on the woman's command. She hadn't wanted to take off her clothes, but she was afraid the woman might make her, and might come into the bathroom with her. She hadn't done that. She only made Juanita hand out her jeans, jacket, and sweat shirt, her bra, panties, and socks. She hadn't seen her sneakers since they brought her here.

She knew now that this was a loft. The bathroom was fancy-new. So was the kitchen, which didn't have any doors. The living room ran all the way from the studio—the room with the big bed and the statues—to what must be the front of the building. Street noises seemed to come from there, and there must be a very big window with heavy curtains covering it. Threads of light showed at the top and at the floor. A Castro convertible bed, where they must have slept, was open. The woman, who said she must call her Dee, told her the big door was to the elevator and was kept locked. Juanita was pretty sure there had to be a fire escape. But where?

"Come out now, Juanita. I want to fix your hair."

The Puppet

"Could I have my clothes, please?"

"You'll get dressed later. Come on now."

She went out to where the woman motioned her into a chair in front of a mirror. "Can't I get dressed before he comes back?"

"First I want to do up your hair." Dee had a dryer in hand. "Little dark pom-poms might be nice. You could look Japanese. Like a geisha girl."

"Please. I hate this." Juanita tugged at the robe.

"Just be patient. You're going to have beautiful new clothes."

Dee blow-dried her hair to where she could work with it, making little round buns she fastened and then let loose, then fashioned again. "Very pretty, my little geisha."

Juanita's fear was getting bad again. She almost wished the man would come. They might have another fight, a long one. When her mother and father fought, she could run away and hide. Where could she run and hide here? She'd make a dash for the big window and pound on it. She would jump up and down. But people would point and laugh and wouldn't do anything. Unless the man came and tried to give her the needle and she fought him right there in the window. Maybe then.

"A penny for your thoughts." Dee smiled at her in the mirror and then looked at herself. "How I wish I was young like you again."

"Don't let him stick the needle in me anymore."

"Over my dead body."

Juanita felt a little more secure and tried once more, "Couldn't I have my clothes back now?"

"No, dear. I've already put them in the garbage disposal."

In the early afternoon, with the help of Vendor Licensing

71

and Traffic Control, Detective Russo located the Greystone Puppets truck. It was impounded in the Twelfth Avenue lot for illegal parking overnight. According to the gatekeeper, the owner had arrived early that morning, but without enough money to pay both fine and storage. He was due back within the hour. Otherwise he'd owe the city another hundred dollars for storage. Julie took what money she had in the house and waited outdoors for the squad car to pick her up. Where she had used to carry a pocketful of coins for blind beggars and street musicians, she now carried dollar bills for the homeless.

She and the two precinct officers Russo had commandeered examined the truck. It was locked up tight, but that didn't mean much, given its condition. As one of the cops said, it was hard to tell what breed it was. They could see the skeleton of a stage set on a platform that probably rolled out onto the tailgate. There was a trunk marked COSTUMES and some painted scenery scaled to the stage. But no puppets.

Very soon a little man with a wisp of a moustache, hollow cheeks, and great melancholy eyes, came up lugging a duffel bag. He showed the cops his receipt from the city. "I had to hock my puppets. They're my kids! My goddam living."

"I'll help you if you can help me," Julie said. She didn't look as though she had much to help with, in sneakers and raincoat. But as soon as she started to describe Juanita she was in charge. She soon had the puppeteer wagging his head. He remembered the girl, all right. "She kept asking me questions— did I make the puppets myself, did I make them out of old dolls. Could she make them. She wanted to know where I was going next. 'Florida,' I says. 'I don't want them to catch cold.' When she saw I was putting her on—the saddest look I ever saw." Then he was jolted aware. "She's come up missing?"

"Since five o'clock last night."

"I was there on the street till ten. But listen: there was this woman I thought at first was the kid's mother. She was telling her about puppets. I was changing the act, see. I got three different acts. . . ."

Julie waited out his setting the scene. One of the cops activated a pocket recorder.

"Somewhere in there I got the idea this dame was a con artist. I don't mean I thought it exactly. It just crossed my mind. She was like playing to me too. That's what kept the youngster interested. She watched to see if I was interested. That kid's no fool. The redhead was telling about this old theater she was renovating and how she was collecting puppets that could make like singers. . . ."

"Where? Did she say where it was?"

"No, ma'am. Not to me, she didn't, and I'll tell you this, she knew about as much about puppets as I know about King Tut. But that's where I lost touch. I got a hand puppet that's my buddy. Whenever we get enough people around, Andy and I pass the hat. It's a living. I guess you could call it a living."

"What else about Juanita?"

He shrugged. "One minute they were there, gone the next. That's how it is when you're playing the street."

The police pressed him for a description of the redheaded woman. Then Julie asked him if he thought the theater she spoke about might be a real place.

"Could be."

"Nearby?"

Again he shrugged. Then: "I don't think that kid would go with her anyplace she couldn't walk to."

A buzzer signaled Danny's return. While the elevator

groaned its way up, Juanita glanced toward the heavily draped window at the front of the loft. Dee clamped her fingers around the girl's wrist. "Don't you even think of it! Do you want to get killed?"

Juanita, still in the silken robe, gathered it tighter in front of her. It didn't have any buttons. She tried not to see herself in the mirror because it wasn't really her. Dee had made her up to look oriental. But she watched in the mirror for the elevator's arrival. When it stopped, Dee had to unlock the door to let Danny in. He took the key from her and locked it again.

"So?" Dee wanted to know.

He didn't answer. He came near and stared at Juanita in the mirror. He made a face like he was going to throw up. "What've you done to her? And what in hell is she doing out of the studio?"

"We needed a bath."

"Then *we* need another bath. She looks like a midget's whore."

"Fun-nee. Did you get what you went for?"

"No. The answer is no. Dee, she's supposed to look like an angel. That's why you fell in love with her."

"Oh, shut up."

"I got a contact. That's all I got and I'm going to go see him as soon as you and I straighten some things out."

"Danny, how much time do you think we have?"

"Maybe we don't have any. This town ought to be the best. But it's the worst yet. Get her inside there so we can talk."

Confined again in the studio, Juanita put her ear to the frame of the door, then to the keyhole. Then she lay down on the floor and tried to hear from under the door, but only the sound of their voices reached her, going away as though to the front of the building. A new sound startled her until she realized it was her stomach growling. She'd promised Dee she would eat. She knew Dee liked her. That's what made Danny mad. But there wasn't any food. Dee looked in the cupboards and the fridge. How could they live someplace with no food in the house? They didn't live here. It was like a hotel, only it was a loft they rented. Their suitcases were on the floor, open, with clothes falling out of them. They'd rented from an artist, which was why Danny wasn't supposed to touch anything in the studio.

She sat on the edge of a chair and wound her feet around its legs. The dressing gown smelled of perfume and sweat. She wished they'd start fighting again so she could hear them. If they didn't have any time, would they go away and leave her locked in this room with the bucket and the big bed? She hated beds more than most things. Her mother and father fought a lot about beds, and her mother had boyfriends she didn't think Juanita or Papa knew about. Papa didn't. She did. She knew that was why her mother let her go when she said she was going to Elena's. She had a date with a boyfriend. Juanita thought of the kids getting on her about the flyers—"What's pornography, Juanita? How come you know so much about it?" She knew it was dirty pictures, but she wasn't going to say it to them. She felt herself going sick again, scared. She tried to think of Julie. Julie would really try to find her. Maybe she'd find the puppet man. He could tell her about Dee. But what else? She hadn't seen Danny before she walked into the old building with the hand-painted sign on the door: PUPPET SHOW INSIDE. Julie walked a lot and she might find it.

Juanita began to walk then, too. Round and round the room she went, barefoot, the silk gown dragging the floor. Finally she entered the alcove where the statues stood around like people at a funeral. There were other things, half-finished bodies, heads. She recognized the smell of clay. Tools and brushes and tubes of paint lay on a table. There was a painting on a three-legged stand, and other paintings were stacked in racks. This was where Danny wasn't supposed to touch anything. She came on several camera cases then, and something rolled up with metal legs sticking out. There were two flat boxes with straps that were marked FILM. These things belonged to Danny, she felt sure, not to the artist. Danny said the light wasn't any good. He was going to take her picture, and he wanted her to look like an angel. That didn't sound like Danny. She'd have thought he would want her to look like a whore.

Julie was in luck when she reached the Actors Forum. A session had just ended. Nobody there knew much about puppets, but when she'd given the actors and apprentices the story, most of them volunteered to organize a street-by-street search of old West Side buildings in which a puppet theater might now be playing or where appropriate renovation might be under way. They would all go first to precinct headquarters and coordinate with the police. "Mind you," Julie cautioned, "the real puppeteer said the woman didn't know anything about puppets. It was probably a story made up to lure the youngster. She's eleven years old and she's pretty. What else can I tell you?"

"We'll find her, sister." Nuba Bradley, a tall, black actor who seemed to have grown three inches with the current hairstyle, bent almost in two to kiss her cheek.

Reggie Bauer hung back to talk to Julie while the others got under way. Slight, blond, and brittle, Reggie knew New York society from the Bowery to the bridge tables; these were where, it was said, he made enough money to support himself as an actor. "You don't think for a minute it's got anything to do with puppets, do you?"

Julie waited.

"Do you want my scenario?"

"Not if it's too far out. Of course, I want it."

"Kid porn."

"What does that mean?" She knew well enough. Or thought she did, but she hoped it wasn't so.

"Child pornography. The lady was shopping for innocence, the real thing. In the meantime, either she's got a partner for her or somebody's out there looking for an experienced young dude to match her up with."

Julie didn't question him on his expertise. She thought she knew how he came by it. Except that Reggie was gay. The thought must have shone through her eyes. He said, "A lot of it's faked, you know, especially the pleasure."

"How would they find a boy like that? Where?"

"Through somebody in the business. Somebody knows somebody who likes boys. A certain amount of trust is involved in the transaction."

"Oh, my God," Julie said. "Maybe I know someone myself."

Juanita stood beneath the skylight and turned around slowly. On tiptoe she could see what looked like the top of a barrel. Bringing one of the chairs to stand on, she could see that it was a water tower. She could see other buildings and a lot of sky. She could also see where water leaked in around the skylight. If she could get up there, she might be able to push the window out.

She went back to the door and listened. She couldn't hear anything except faraway car horns and the rumble of the city much as it sounded when she was home alone in the daytime. Maybe they'd both gone out. Maybe they'd already gone and left her. And left the camera and everything? She didn't think so. She wasn't going to let them photograph her without her clothes on. Not unless he used the needle again. This time she'd kick it out of his hand or kick him where she knew it would hurt most. "Over my dead body," Dee had said. But Dee was afraid of him too.

She took the painting off the three-legged stand. Even if she could step on the stand, it wouldn't be high enough. Again she listened at the door. They'd gone out to lunch, she decided, and Dee would bring back something for her. It had to be after lunchtime. As quietly as she could she pulled the table under the skylight. The stand just fit on top of it. The dressing gown made it hard for her to climb, and she knew it was going to get in her way if she got high enough to try to move the window. But it had pockets. She found a paint-smeared knife and a chisel, which she pocketed. She also took a hammer and tied it around her waist with the sash of the robe. She tried not to think of Danny, but in spite of herself she imagined him unlocking the door just as she stepped from the chair onto the table. She began to melt again with fear.

"No!" she cried aloud without meaning to. She waited. Nothing happened. She could not climb up on the stand. The ledge she wanted to step onto was too high. She pulled the chair up onto the table, but in doing it she nudged one of the legs of the stand and the whole thing clattered to the floor. Not a sound came from the other side of the door. This time, after she'd set up the stand and placed the chair beneath it, she boosted herself up without tumbling the works. She waited and listened. There were sounds she hadn't heard before in the building, noise like heat coming up in the pipes, machinery sounds that might be the elevator. But it never seemed to arrive. Her heartbeat was too loud to hear much else. She made it safely up onto the chair. She could see the twin towers of the Board of Trade Buildings. She was in lower Manhattan. SoHo. Of course: where the artists were. She got one foot sidewise onto the ledge and tested to see if it would hold her. It seemed to, but when she tried to lift the other foot the stand wobbled and collapsed. She missed the chair and fell and, flailing, brought the chair down after her. Before she knew whether or not she was hurt, Dee threw open the door and came running to her. Juanita tried to pull the robe close around her.

"I wouldn't've believed it! He was right, I shouldn't've left you alone. Let me look at your face." On her knees, Dee examined her face, touched her eyes, nose, lips. "Say ouch if it hurts."

Juanita determined not to say ouch no matter how much it hurt. She managed to loosen the hammer and tie the sash around her. Dee felt down her arms and pulled the robe open to see her middle. Juanita closed it again. She knew there would be bruises where she'd hit the table, but she didn't make a sound when Dee touched the sore spots.

Dee got to her feet and pulled the girl up. "You're lucky in more ways than one, you little fool. Let's put these things back where they were. I promise I won't tell Danny if you promise to do what you're told from now on. Promise me?" She gave the girl a shake.

Juanita was trying not to cry. She did hurt, but she forced a big smile and nodded what could be taken for a promise. She had lost the chisel on the way down, but she could feel the knife stuck deep in the pocket of the robe.

Julie stopped at the shop to see if any message had come through her service. Most of the calls pertained to business. She put them on hold. Several Women Against Pornography members had joined the neighborhood search. Mrs. Rodriguez had called twice. Julie ran upstairs. The woman had heard nothing. Her husband had gone to the police station to wait. There were a lot of *Perdidas* in her lamentation.

Julie walked the four blocks to Kevin Bourke's electrical shop on Eighth Avenue. Mr. Bourke was one of the first people she'd met after moving into the shop. He loaned a friend of hers some lamps to help decorate it. He had lived in the neighborhood all his life, he attended St. Malachy's where the Catholic actors went, supported the Irish Theater, and looked a bit like Sean O'Casey, whose plays he admired fervently. He had been in trouble when Julie met him, on the complaint of a boy who turned out later to have been a prostitute. Julie might not have been so direct if her mission had been less urgent.

Mr. Bourke looked at her sadly over the top of his rimless glasses. "I'll not waste your time asking why it was me you came to. Do you know how many years I've been in therapy to amend that fall from grace?"

"I wouldn't have come to you at all if I knew anyone else to go to."

"You're not alone, and I'd rather have you remember than most of those who do. Thank God, I'll soon be an old man."

Julie thought he already was.

"I wish I could help you, Julie, but I've not been hospitable to that kind of visitor for a long time."

"I understand and I'm sorry I came, Mr. Bourke."

Mercifully, a customer entered the shop and she could get away. She plunged out the door and almost collided with a street person who stepped back to admire the window he had cleaned of a car illegally parked at the curb. What could he see, she wondered, the windows all blacked out. She glanced back at the license plate—California. All that sunshine they wouldn't let in the windows.

The Puppet

Juanita ate. Ordinarily she loved Chinese food, but now she could hardly swallow. She had a plan. It came out of the daydreams she often made up about Julie and herself. Dee, she could see, was getting nervous. She walked back and forth waiting for Juanita to finish eating. She stopped and threw a lot of clothes that were lying about into one of the suitcases. She listened for the elevator. She looked at her watch. She was waiting to change Juanita's hairdo. The pom-poms had come undone when she tumbled off the table. Danny didn't want her to look like a geisha girl anyway. Dee wouldn't tell her what a geisha girl was. She knew what an angel was, but she didn't feel like one of them either.

Dee came close and looked at the plate. "Starved, weren't you?"

"Dee, I don't like Danny. Do you?"

The woman gave a surprised laugh. "Not always."

"Are you married to him?"

"We're partners. Does that answer your question?"

"You just live together, right?"

"Right. If you've had enough to eat, go sit in front of the mirror." Dee took the plate to the sink and scraped and rinsed it.

Juanita sat on the bench at the dressing table and drew the robe tightly around her. She watched Dee approach, drying her hands on a dishtowel. "Why don't you split from him? I mean, everybody does it. My mother and father talk about it all the time."

"Stop talking so much and go wash your face. You got some dirt on your cheek."

The dirt was a sore spot. Juanita saw that her plan wasn't going to work, but she had to try anyway. She didn't have any other. "Dee, what if you and I ran away before he gets back?

81

He's mean to you, too. I'll bet he beats up on you, right? Couldn't we go someplace and make a real puppet show?"

Dee folded her arms and looked down at her for a long time. "Don't you ever want to see your parents again?"

"Not really." She gave her shoulders a shrug.

"You're a conniving little bitch, Juanita. Did you think I'd fall for a line like that? Get up and take off the robe."

"No." The knife was in the pocket. "I don't want to take it off, please."

Dee came up behind her and tried to wrench the robe from her shoulders. Juanita clung to the lapels. But when she could hold on no longer, she wriggled round on the bench and swung at Dee with all her might. The red hair leaped off the woman's head and plopped on the floor like a bird's nest. Juanita jumped for the wig and ran with it to the front of the loft. She tried to get through the heavy curtains, but Dee was too close. She threw herself at the girl and brought her to the floor.

Julie was near despair when she got home. Reggie Bauer's scenario could be due entirely to his own aberration. Great. But if that were so, what to do next? Once more she checked in with her service. A call had come from Nuba Bradley of the Actors Forum. They had found a sign saying PUPPET SHOW INSIDE. A homeless person was incorporating the sign into his wind shelter. A building-by-building search was under way. Julie called Detective Russo. He confirmed the search and the discovery of a pair of sneakers that could belong to the missing subject. "You might as well know the worst," Russo summarized. "They're bringing in a squatter from the building across the way. He watched two people load something into a station wagon about eight o'clock last night. We'll try to improve his memory, but all there is so far—a black wagon. Even the windows looked black to him."

Julie phoned Kevin Bourke. The line was busy. She had left his place only ten minutes before and had not even taken off her coat. She ran back to and up Eighth Avenue. A cabbie pulled alongside her and tapped his horn. She signaled that she wanted him, but kept on running. She could see the black car at the curb outside Bourke's shop. Not a cop in sight, not even a meter maid.

Mr. Bourke stepped out of the shop with the customer, who looked at his watch and poked a cautionary finger at Bourke. He strode to the wagon and pushed the street person out of his way. When he drove off, the cabbie took over the spot.

"I tried to call you," Bourke said. "You'd have known what I meant."

"I got a bead on him," the cabbie said as Julie jumped in. The wagon turned left at the stoplight. The late afternoon traffic was building. On Ninth Avenue it was at a crawl. The wagon stayed near the middle lane; the cabbie, to be sure the car he followed didn't opt for the Lincoln Tunnel, kept to the fire lane himself.

Julie made a note of the California license number and asked the driver if he couldn't radio a message to the police.

"No, ma'am. I'm a gypsy. I don't have that intercom stuff. But don't you worry none, he ain't going to get away."

But he almost did get away, slipping into a tunnel lane and then spurting out of it instead of turning west. He ran the light and went free while the westbound traffic closed in ahead of Julie's cab.

"He sure drives California style," the driver said. "What're you after him for?"

"I'm pretty sure he helped kidnap an eleven-year-old girl."

The cabbie shot out on the orange light and within four blocks of progressive lights was headlights-to-back-bumper with the wagon. "I'll ram him if you want me to."

"For God's sake, no. I want to see where he's going."

At Fourteenth Street the wagon made a couple of starts in the wrong direction before taking off down Hudson. Now Julie was afraid he'd know the cab was following him. At Bleecker and Bethune he came to a full stop at the playground gate.

"Keep going," Julie said.

But the driver in the wagon rolled down his window and signaled. The cabbie stopped alongside him.

"How in hell do I get to Houston Street from here?" He pronounced it like a Texan.

"Follow me," the cabbie said, and then to Julie as he led the way through the Greenwich Village maze, "See my point?"

The cabbie crossed Houston, a one-way street going west at that point, and signaled the wagon. But the wagon turned east, the wrong way.

The cabbie swore and ran two lights to get back on Houston by way of Sixth Avenue where Houston was two-way by then. They kept their distance as the wagon slowed down at every intersection, the driver looking for his street. He turned in at Wooster. But Wooster, they discovered when they got there, was blocked this side of Prince Street. A movie shooting there? So where were the trailers, where were the cops? The cops loved movies. Julie overpaid the cabbie and took her chances on foot. She knew SoHo pretty well.

She soon spotted the black wagon parked tight against a high wire fence midblock. The driver was wriggling across the front seat to get out on the passenger side. He went to the back and unloaded a couple of high-wattage lamps and a reflector. Could be they were on rental from Mr. Bourke. The man started up the street with them on the opposite side to the crowd. Julie stayed on the crowd's side, but at the fringe. At last the distant wail of approaching police. Two things happened at once: the man set down the lamps and reflector and, ignoring the crowd, took out his keys to unlock a door, and the crowd let out a collective cry, "Look! Look!"

Julie looked. A woman was dancing nude in the third-floor picture window. Not dancing, but jumping up and down, flailing her arms, and not a woman. It was Juanita.

Julie plunged across the street, waving to the girl and calling out, "Juanita!"

Some of the crowd moved with and past her. Interpreting for themselves, they caught hold of the man, pushed him from one to another, and pulled at his clothes. The multilocked loft door swung open. The redheaded woman took a step into the street, then tried to retreat inside the building again. When no one else took hold of her, Julie lunged and grappled her to the ground. The crowd loved it. The police came finally, swinging their nightsticks to disperse the crowd.

Julie and Juanita rode home in the chief inspector's car after they had stopped at One Police Plaza, to swear out the necessary complaints. There were things Juanita would not or could not talk about—mostly her fear and what she'd imagined might happen to her, but she liked to tell the action parts, especially how, when Dee had chased and caught her, she clung to the front window drapes and brought them down on top of Dee and her. By the time Dee had found her wig, Juanita was dancing in the window. Oh, yes, she insisted, she *was* dancing.

In time, police across the country fleshed out the chronicle of Dee and Danny, a horror story. They would arrive in a city, sublet quarters, recruit local talent, film, and move on. They supplied a flourishing market in underground cassettes. The true horror was not only in their corruption of the innocent, but in the despair in which they left the corrupted. These unfortunates rarely went home again and almost never broke their silence on the street.

Justina

Mary Ryan was certainly not homeless. She had lived in the Willoughby for forty-three years. Once it had been a residential hotel occupied mainly by show folk, people who worked in or about the theater at subsistence or slightly higher level. Recently it had been renovated into a stylish cooperative, but with a few small inside pockets, you might say, of people like Mrs. Ryan, who were allowed to remain on as renters by the grace of a qualified managerial charity: after all, what can you put in an inside pocket? Besides tax rebates.

The neighborhood—the West Forties of Manhattan—had gone, in Mrs. Ryan's time, from respectable working-class to shabby and drug-pocked misery and back again to a confusing mix of respectability, affluence, and decay. But through all the changes, the area had remained a neighborhood, with people who had lived there all their lives loyal to one another, to the shops who served them, to church and school, and who were, by and large, tolerant of the unfortunates and the degraded who came and went among them with the inevitability of time and tide.

As Mrs. Ryan got out of the elevator that January morning, she saw the nun backing off from the doorman. Louis seemed to be trying to persuade her to go out of the building by demonstrating how it could be done. He would prance three or four feet ahead of her toward the door and beckon her to follow him. The nun would take a step away from him deeper into the lobby.

Mrs. Ryan had seen the nun in the building before, and

she had seen her on the street, always hurrying, always laden with nondescript bundles and shopping bags. She was tall and lean and wore a habit such as most orders had stepped out of years before. Nor could Mrs. Ryan associate her garb with that of any order in her long religious acquaintanceship. "Is there any way I can help you, Sister?" she asked when she came abreast of the nun and the doorman.

"Better you can help me," Louis said, pleading with empty hands. "The super says she's not to come in, but she is in."

"You ought to show respect, Louis. A Sister is a Sister. You don't speak of her as *she*."

The nun gazed at Mrs. Ryan with large china-blue eyes that were full of pleading. "Can he put me out if I'm waiting for a friend?"

"Certainly not," Mrs. Ryan said.

Louis started to walk away in disgust and then turned back. "Miss Brennan left the building an hour ago in her nurse's uniform. Wouldn't you say it would be a long wait till she comes back, Mrs. Ryan?"

"Sheila Brennan is a friend of mine," Mrs. Ryan said. "If she said she'll be back, she'll be back. Would you like to come up to my place for a cup of tea, Sister? We can phone down to Louis and see if she comes in."

"How very kind of you, Mrs. Ryan. I would love a cup of tea." Moving with more grace than would be thought possible in the heavy, square-toed shoes, the nun collected two shopping bags from among the poinsettias. Mrs. Ryan hadn't noticed them. Whether Louis had, she couldn't know. He was standing, his back to them, looking out onto the street and springing up and down on his toes.

In the elevator, Mrs. Ryan surveyed her guest surreptitiously. She wore a full black skirt all the way to her shoe-tops and a jacket that seemed more Chinese than Christian. It buttoned clear up under her chin. The crucifix she wore was an ivory figure on what looked to be a gold or bronze cross. It put Mrs. Ryan in mind of one she had once noticed on a black man who, according to her friend Julie Hayes, was a pimp. For just that instant she wondered if she had done the right thing in inviting the nun upstairs. What reassured her was an association from her youth in Ireland: there was a smell to the nun only faintly unpleasant, as of earth or the cellar, but remembered all Mrs. Ryan's life from the Sisters to whom she had gone in infant school. Alas, it was the smell of poverty.

Over her head of shaggy brown hair, the nun wore a thin veil that came down to her breast. It was not much of a veil, but there was not much breast to her, either. She said her name was Sister Justina and her order was the Sisters of Our Lady of Hope, of whom there were so few left each was allowed to choose her own ministry: most, Sister Justina said, worked among the poor and the illiterate, and often lived with them, as she herself did.

What Mrs. Ryan called her apartment was a single room into which she had crammed a life, and which she had for many years shared with a dachshund recently gone to where the good dogs go. A life-size picture of Fritzie hung on the wall among a gallery of actors and directors and theater entrepreneurs. "There's not a face up there you'd recognize today, but I knew them all," she said, coming out of the bathroom where she'd put the kettle on to boil on the electric plate.

The nun was gazing raptly at the faded photographs. "Were you an actor?"

"I was an usher," Mrs. Ryan said proudly.

"Theater people are the most generous I've ever begged from. I am a beggar, you know," Justina said with a simplicity that touched Mrs. Ryan to the core. There was something luminous about her. She spoke softly, her voice throaty and low, but an educated voice.

"The Franciscans—I always give to the Franciscans," Mrs. Ryan said. It was the only begging order she knew.

"I feel closer to St. Francis myself than to any other saint," Sister Justina said. "Sometimes I pray for a mission among birds and animals, and then I'm reminded that pigeons are birds, and that rats and mice must have come off the ark as well as the loftier creatures. But I think I do my best work among the poor who ought never to have come to the city at all. They are the really lost ones." She was sitting at the foot of the daybed, rubbing her hands together. The color had risen to her cheeks.

Mrs. Ryan thought of tuberculosis. "Don't you have a shawl, Sister?"

"I'm warm enough inside, thank you. I have so many calls to make, would you think it ungrateful of me to run off without waiting for tea?"

Or Sheila Brennan, Mrs. Ryan thought. But she had grown accustomed to visitors finding her apartment both claustrophobic and too warm. "The electric plate is terrible slow," she said, making an excuse for her guest's departure.

"You're very kind," the nun said. Her eyes welled up. "God bless!" She gathered a shopping bag in each hand and went flapping down the hall like a bird that couldn't get off the ground.

A few minutes later Mrs. Ryan was downstairs again, about to resume her trip to the Seminal Thrift Shop. She lingered near the elevators until Louis went outdoors to look for a cab for one of the tenants with liquid assets, as Sheila Brennan liked to say of the coop owners. She was not in the mood for a lecture from Louis, who couldn't stand street people, even if they belonged to a religious order. She was almost to the corner of Ninth Avenue when a gust of wind came up, whirling the dust before it. She turned her back, and so it was that she saw Sister Justina emerge from the service or basement entrance of the Willoughby. She clutched her veil against the wind and hurried toward Eighth Avenue, the opposite direction from Mrs. Ryan. And without her shopping bags.

Julie had the feeling that Mrs. Ryan had been waiting for her—not exactly lying in wait, but keeping an eye out for her to appear, either coming to or going from her ground-floor apartment on Forty-fourth Street. Theirs was a friendship of several years, recently broken and more recently mended. Julie still kept the tin box of dog biscuits in case the old lady appeared one day with another Fritzie in tow.

Mrs. Ryan came halloing across the street ahead of a rush of traffic. "Do you have a few minutes, Julie? There's something I need your advice on."

Julie had a few minutes. She was of the conviction that a gossip columnist hustled best who hustled least. Her visit to the rehearsal of *Uptown Downtown* could wait. She unlocked the door and led the way back into her apartment-office.

"Do you remember the day we put down the deposit here, Julie?"

Julie remembered, but it seemed a long time ago, her brief sortie into reading and advising. Sheer mischief, she'd say of it now. Now "the shop," as she'd always called it, was comfortable to live in and equipped as well with the electronics of her trade. She had learned to use the computer and rarely went near the *New York Daily* office at all.

"Friend Julie," Mrs. Ryan said, her voice lush with reminiscence. Then: "You have such good instincts about people. I want to tell you about a nun I met this morning, a beautiful person, the most spiritual eyes you ever saw." Mrs. Ryan didn't exactly proselyte, but she did propagate the faith.

"I'm not great on nuns," Julie said, and the phrase "a nun and a neck" popped into her mind. Where it had come from she had no idea.

"They're not much different from you and me," Mrs. Ryan said.

Julie raised her eyebrows.

"Her name is Sister Justina," Mrs. Ryan said, and told the story of their encounter.

"Are you sure she's a nun?" was Julie's first question.

"I'd swear to it."

"What does Miss Brennan say about her?"

"Sheila's on the day shift this week—I wouldn't go to the hospital looking for her about this. It's the shopping bags that bother me. What did she do with them?"

"And what was in them? You've got to think about drugs, Mrs. Ryan."

"It crossed my mind, may the Lord forgive me, and I suppose, to be honest, I'd have to say that's why I've come to you."

"It would seem she wanted most to get into the Willoughby," Julie reconstructed. "She tried to make it on Miss Brennan's name and then you came along. It looks as though her purpose was to deliver the shopping bags, but without the doorman or you knowing who she was delivering them to."

Mrs. Ryan agreed reluctantly.

"How did she get past the doorman in the first place?"

"She must have slipped in the way I slipped out—when he was handing someone into a cab."

"Were the bags heavy or light?"

"They flopped along, not heavy, not light."

"And why go out the basement door? Why not sail past the doorman with her head in the air?"

"Ah, she wasn't the type. She told me right out that she was a beggar—but in the way St. Francis was a beggar."

"Funny about that cross," Julie said. "I saw Goldie the other day. 'Miz Julie, I'm straight as a flagpole,' " she mimicked. "He even gave me his business card."

"Was he wearing the crucifix?" Mrs. Ryan asked disapprovingly.

Julie grinned. "I doubt it. He was wearing Brooks Brothers." She took a mug of tea from the micro-oven and set it before the older woman.

"Fancy," Mrs. Ryan said, "and me still using an electric plate." The tea was "instant" and she hated it.

Julie wondered how many like Mrs. Ryan and Sheila Brennan were still living in the Willoughby. "What was the name of your actor friend? Remember he took us down to the basement that time to look up his old notices in the trunk room?"

"Jack Carroll. He's gone now, God rest him. He was a lovely man but a terrible bore." Mrs. Ryan drank the tea down, trying not to taste it.

"That was one spooky place," Julie said. "Cobwebs and leaky pipes, and the smell of mold and old clothes when he opened the trunk."

"It's all changed down there now with the renovation. The old part's been sealed off. There's brand new washers and dryers in the new section and it's as bright as daylight."

"She wouldn't be stealing from the dryers, would she? To give to the poor, of course."

"She would not," Mrs. Ryan said indignantly. Then, having to account to herself for the shopping bags, she added, "Besides, she'd be taking a terrible chance of being caught."

"But wouldn't that account for her going out without the bags—the fear that someone had seen her?"

"Oh, dear, I hope she doesn't come looking for me now to let her back in," Mrs. Ryan said. "I could be out in the cold myself. I'm on severance with the management. They pretend not to know I cook in my room."

"Mrs. Ryan," Julie said, "why don't you forget I said that? It's wild. I have a wicked imagination. And I'd stop worrying about the nun if I were you. She got into the building before you came along—she's not your responsibility."

Mrs. Ryan looked at her reproachfully. Then her face lit up. "Julie, I'd love you to meet her. I'll bring her around someday if I can get her to come and let you judge for yourself."

Sheila Brennan stuck her stockinged feet out for Mrs. Ryan to see. "Will you look at my ankles? You'd think it was the height of summer." The ankles were indeed swollen.

"It's being on them all day," Mrs. Ryan said. "Put them up on the couch while I pour the tea."

Sheila was younger than Mrs. Ryan, a plain, solid woman who dreaded the day of her retirement from St. Jude's Hospital. "The first I saw of Sister Justina was when she visited someone brought into the hospital with frostbite during that bad spell in December. You know the woman who tries to sell yesterday's newspapers on the corner of Fifty-first Street? The police brought her in half frozen. I told the nun that if she'd come to the Willoughby when I got off duty, and if she could promise me the woman would wear it, I'd give her a fisherman's shirt my brother brought me from Donegal. It was foolish of me to put a condition to it and what she said made me ashamed of myself. 'If she doesn't wear it, I will,' she said. I've been asking around of this one and that one to give her their castoffs ever since."

"So she's on the up and up," Mrs. Ryan said and put the

teacup and saucer in her friend's hand. "But what was she doing in the Willoughby basement?"

"God knows, Mary. She may just have pushed the wrong elevator-button and wound up there."

Julie and her imagination, Mrs. Ryan thought.

Sheila Brennan's explanation satisfied Mrs. Ryan because she wanted to be satisfied with it. And she did believe the nun to be a true sister to the poor. She saw her again later that week. Mrs. Ryan was herself in the habit now of taking her principal meal at the Seniors Center in St. Malachy's basement, where she got wholesome food in a cheerful environment at a price she could afford. Afterward, that afternoon, she went upstairs to the Actors Chapel and there she encountered Sister Justina kneeling in a back pew, her shopping bags at her sides.

"Sister—" Mrs. Ryan whispered hoarsely.

The nun jumped as though startled out of deep meditation and upset one of the shopping bags. Out tumbled a variety of empty plastic cups.

Mrs. Ryan went into the pew and helped her collect them, saying how sorry she was to have startled her. The containers, she noted, were reasonably clean, but certainly not new. "All I wanted to say," she explained, "is that I have a friend who would like to meet you. Her name is Julie Hayes. She's a newspaper columnist. She writes about all kinds of people, and she's very good to the needy."

"I've heard of her," the nun said without enthusiasm.

Mrs. Ryan realized she had taken the wrong tack. "Do you mind coming out to the vestibule for a minute? I can't get used to talking in church."

In the vestibule, she modified her description of Julie. "It's true that she helps people. She's even helped the police now and then. I know of at least two murders she's helped them solve. It would take me all day to tell you about her. But, Sister, she's as needy in her way as you are in yours. You both have a great deal to give, but what would you do if you didn't have takers?"

The nun laughed and then clutched at her throat to stop the cough the laugh had started. "Someday," she said when she could get her breath.

"Someday soon," Mrs. Ryan said. "She lives a few doors from the Actors Forum. You know where that is. I helped her find the place. In those days she called herself Friend Julie."

"Friend Julie," the nun repeated with a kind of recognition. Then: "I must hurry, Mrs. Ryan. They throw out the food if I don't get there in time." She ran down the steps with her bags of containers to collect the leftovers from the Seniors' midday meal.

"Nowadays it's just plain Julie Hayes," Mrs. Ryan called after her.

Julie never doubted that Mrs. Ryan would arrive one day with the nun by the hand, but what she hadn't expected was the nun's arrival alone. She didn't like unannounced visitors, but the ring of the doorbell was urgent and came with a clatter she presently attributed to the nun's use of the cross as a knocker. In fact, it was by the cross—an ivory figure on gold—that she recognized her as Mrs. Ryan's friend. She took off the safety latch and opened the door.

"Friend Julie, I need your help."

"Has something happened to Mrs. Ryan?"

"No," the nun said. "Please?"

Julie relocked the door after the nun and led the way through the apartment. She was trying to remember the nun's name.

"Mrs. Ryan has nothing to do with this, I give my word," the nun said. "She said you wanted to meet me, but that's not why I'm here. I'm Sister Justina."

Julie motioned her into a chair and seated herself across the coffee table from her. She didn't say anything. She just waited for the pitch. It was those big blue eyes, she thought, that had got to Mrs. Ryan.

"All I need to tell you about my mission, I think, is that I try to find temporary shelter for street people who are afraid of institutional places. It's a small person-to-person endeavor, but I've had very good luck until now. I've been keeping two people hidden away at night and in bad weather in an abandoned section of the Willoughby basement."

"You're kidding," Julie said.

"I wish I were." The nun thrust her clasped hands between her knees. "I went to leave them a meal this afternoon." She took a deep breath. "One man was gone and the other one was dead. His skull was smashed in!" Her amazing eyes were filling.

"You're lucky it wasn't you, Sister."

"I don't consider myself lucky."

"Have you gone to the police?"

Justina shook her head. "That's why I came to you. Mrs. Ryan said you've helped the police—"

"Let's forget what Mrs. Ryan says. *You* have to go to the police. You can't just close up that part of the basement again on a dead man as though it was a tomb."

"I don't want to do that. I only wish I could have got poor Tim out of the city in time. He wanted to go, but he was afraid." She looked at Julie pleadingly. "I want to do what I have to do, but I can't."

"I'll go with you if that will help," Julie offered.

"Would you go *for* me?"

"No. If you don't show up and take the responsibility for trespassing or whatever it was, Mrs. Ryan and Miss Brennan could be evicted, and where would they find a place to live?"

Justina shook her head. "Nothing like this has ever happened to me."

"I'll say it again, then: you're lucky."

"Yes, I suppose I am," the nun said with what sounded like heavy irony. "The habit I wear has been my salvation, my hope in life." She drew a long shuddering breath. "Julie, I'm a man."

For a while Julie said nothing. She was remembering where the phrase "a nun and a neck" had come from—the poet Rilke commenting on one of Picasso's acrobats: "The son of a nun and a neck."

"You can use the phone there on my desk if you want to, Sister," she said.

"Thank you," Justina said. She got up. "Who do I call?"

"Try nine-one-one," Julie said.

The nun identified herself to the police dispatcher as Sister Justina, told of a body in the basement of the Willoughby Apartments, and promised to wait herself at the service entrance to the building.

She gave them the address.

When Mrs. Ryan dropped in at Billy McGowan's pub for her afternoon glass of lager, Detective Dom Russo was telling of the down-and-outer his detail had taken into custody that afternoon for trying to pass a kinky hundred-dollar bill. Nobody had seen its like since before World War Two. Billy had the first dollar he made in America framed and hung above the bar. He pointed it out to the custom.

"They don't make 'em like that any more," the detective said, wanting to get on with his story. "This Bingo claimed first off that he found it, just picked it up off the street. We turned him loose and put a tail on him. You know where the old railroad tracks used to run under Forty-fourth Street? He made a beeline for a hole in the fence, slid down the embankment, and led us straight to where he'd hidden three plastic containers in an old burnt-out stove. I don't need to tell you—the containers were stuffed with all this old-fashioned money."

Someone down the bar wisecracked that that was the best kind. But at the mention of plastic containers, Mrs. Ryan could not swallow her beer.

"We took him in again. This time around, he said he found the money right there in the oven of this old stove. He intended to turn it over to the police, of course," Russo repeated sarcastically, "only first he wanted to look more respectable and went to the thrift shop with one of the C-notes—a silver certificate, they used to call them."

"He should have gone right to the bank," someone else down the bar said. "They'd trade it in—dollar for dollar."

"No questions asked?" someone wanted to know.

"He should have gone to a collector and made himself some real money," Billy said.

"Look," Russo told them, "you're acting like this guy was kosher. Maybe the *money's* kosher, but he's not. I don't believe for a minute he lucked into all that old cash. Anyway, we'll hold him till we hear from the Feds."

"A developing story, as they say." McGowan moved down the bar to Mrs. Ryan. "Drink up, Mary, and I'll put a head on it for you."

"I'll take a rain check, Billy," she told him. "I've got terrible heartburn." She eased herself off the stool, and by ancient habit looked under it, half expecting Fritzie to be curled up there. Out on the street, she drew several deep breaths of the wintry air. Plastic cups, she told herself, weren't such a rare commodity.

It was almost dark and there were misty halos around the streetlights—and when she turned the corner she could see rainbows of revolving color: police activity outside the Willoughby. She approached near enough to see that the action was concentrated around the basement entrance, whereupon she reversed herself and headed for Julie's as fast as her legs would carry her.

Julie was short on patience at the arrival of Mrs. Ryan. For one thing, she was uneasy about not having followed up on the nun's story. After all, she was in the newspaper business. She ought at least to have called the city desk on a breaking story. Or covered it herself. But she had wanted to give Justina a chance to confront the police on her own. She certainly didn't want to be the person to blow her cover.

When Mrs. Ryan finished giving out her jigsaw of a tale, Julie asked her if she'd seen Sister Justina after they'd met at St. Malachy's.

"I haven't."

"Well, she's been here this afternoon, Mrs. Ryan. The police are at the Willoughby to investigate a murder that took place there in the basement. It's highly possible they'll connect it with your man with the money in the plastic cups."

"Holy Mother of God," Mrs. Ryan said.

"And they'll be looking for witnesses, for accessories."

"Sister Justina?"

"And *her* accessories," Julie said. "Your doorman isn't about to take credit for letting her into the building, is he?"

Mrs. Ryan sat a long while in silence. "Would you mind walking me home, dear? My legs are so weak I'm not sure they'll carry me."

Julie pulled on her coat, put the phone on "Service," and fastened her press card onto the inside flap of her shoulderbag.

Mrs. Ryan got weaker and weaker on the way. She suggested they stop for a brief rest at McGowan's, but Julie put a firm hand beneath the older woman's elbow and propelled her homeward.

By then word of police activity at the Willoughby had reached McGowan's and most of the patrons were there to see what was going on. Julie spotted Detective Russo as he came out of the building on the run. She planted Mrs. Ryan among her McGowan's cronies at the barricade and caught up with him as he was climbing into the back of a squad car.

"Okay if I come along?" she asked, halfway into the car behind him. They were on pretty good terms, considering that they weren't always on the same side.

"Why not?" he said ironically.

By the time they reached the precinct house, she knew how the victim and his assailant had got into that part of the Willoughby. The Environmental Protection Department had ordered a removal of old sewage pipes and part of the wall had been removed, a temporary partition put up in its place. "Like everything else in this town," Russo said, "they get the job half done and move on to the next one."

No mention of the nun. "How did they get into the building in the first place, Dom?" Julie asked.

"How the hell do I know? Somebody must've left the door open. And no wonder. It stinks to high heaven down back where they were. They buried their own shit like animals. That's how they found the body—and the tin box with the money in it."

"The money in the plastic cups you found earlier this afternoon. Do you think there's a connection?"

"You better believe it," Russo said. "The victim had one clutched in his hand when he was clobbered with the tin box."

"How did you know to go to the Willoughby in the first place?"

"We had a phone call," Russo said. "But the complainant didn't show. We'd begun to think it was a hoax—but the smell led us to him. A whole section of the wall—we just leaned on it and Jericho!"

"Jericho," Julie said. "That's nice."

So Justina had vanished. No problem: just get out of the habit and grow a beard. Until now she had carried Justina's confession of identity as a confidence, as though it had been told under a seal. It hadn't, of course, but since Detective Russo and company had the suspect in custody and enough evidence to detain him for a while she decided to keep the matter on hold.

Mrs. Ryan and Sheila Brennan were waiting for Julie when she arrived at Mrs. Ryan's apartment. They seemed less chastened than she thought they ought to be, but there hadn't yet been time for the police to get to them.

"We're expecting them any minute," Mrs. Ryan said. "And we've decided to tell them the truth about Sister."

"And that is?"

"How she got into the building in the first place. How she used us."

Julie felt she was being used herself—that this was a dress rehearsal. "Okay."

"But she would have used anybody to help those she thought needed help." Mrs. Ryan drew a deep breath. "Julie, who would you say all that money belongs to?"

"I wouldn't say." But she was beginning to see a light.

"Sheila and I have a story to tell you. Remember you mentioned Jack Carroll the other day, and his trunk in the basement? Jack lived here for years before Sheila and I ever heard of the Willoughby and he loved to tell stories of the old days— the circus people, the vaudevillians, and the chorus girls. One of his best stories, and God knows he practiced to make it perfect, was about Big Frankie Malloy. When Frankie moved in, the management renovated a whole suite for him. He had tons of money. He had his own barber sent in every day to shave him, he had his meals catered; he was always sending out for this or that, he was a lavish tipper. And the girls, there were plenty of them. But there was something wrong about big Frankie. After he moved in, he never went outdoors again—except once.

"Madge Delaney was his favorite of the girls, and she got booked into the Blue Diamond nightclub just down the street. Frankie went out the night she opened. It was said afterward that the only reason she got the booking was to lure him out. He was shot dead before he ever got to the Blue Diamond."

"Wow," Julie said.

"Don't you think it could be his money that's been hidden away all these years?"

"It's a real possibility," Julie agreed.

"You see why I asked you who it belongs to now."

"I do see," Julie assured her.

Julie's story made page 3 of the bulldog edition of the *New York Daily* and the police, discovering there was no such religious order as the Sisters of Our Lady of Hope, put out an alert for Sister Justina. The Willoughby claimed all of that very old money. It also threatened to sue the contractor

stanchion. The lights flickered on the Christmas tree. The steam pipes hissed and rattled. At a signal from Christopher, Miranda gave a great whang to a Chinese gong. The audience jumped. They were alive.

Christopher announced as the finale the most dangerous feat in his repertoire. The act, he said, had made him famous the world over. He was a dapper man, slight, with hollow cheeks, a sharp nose, pale blue eyes, a thin mustache, and an unmistakable Midwestern accent although he claimed to have grown up in Budapest, Hungary. His hands were graceful and quick and his whole body had a squirrel-like agility. For this trick, however, he stood severely straight and still. He seemed to feed himself, one by one, an entire packet of needles. He grimaced in pain at every swallow. The folding chairs squeaked as his audience sat forward, finally alert. The children's eyes were popping.

"Hush," Miranda said to a house already hushed.

Christopher balled a length of thread and stuffed it into his mouth. In his display of agony, he resembled a Christian martyr often featured on funeral cards. His audience belonged to him. The hundred or so empty chairs no longer mattered. Then, with a silent prayer, he extracted an end of thread from between his tongue and his teeth and carefully drew out a chain of neatly threaded needles. He skipped down the steps and invited a youngster in the front row to look into the cavern of his mouth.

Maggie didn't know how he did it. Nor did she care. It seemed mighty unhygienic. In fact, she hated magic, but she had the only job she could get. The country was in a depression—dust bowls and soup kitchens, Father Coughlin and John L. Lewis, the latter revered in Bluefield, West Virginia, the coal and rail town they were about to pull out of, to head home for Christmas. Home for Maggie was a small town in

Michigan, for Christopher it was Fort Wayne, Indiana. Christmas was two days away.

It was ten past twelve when they hit the highway in Christopher's sedan. It was custom-packed, floorboards to roof, the back seat removed to accommodate his magic, livestock, and luggage. Maggie's luggage consisted of an imitation leather suitcase and a canvas bag of books for which the only room was at her feet. Two spare tires were strapped to the running boards. Those on the car were as bald as the liners inside them. The car gave a thud at every tar-filled crack in the pavement. There was a strong odor of bird dung in the car—Maggie didn't think rabbit droppings smelled—but stronger was the smell of the half onion Christopher had at the ready in case the windshield frosted. It was a cold night and grew colder the higher they went into the mountains. An oval moon rode high. It silvered the hills, etched telegraph poles, slag heaps, and occasional cottages in which the lights were long out. Far down in the valley the railroad tracks shone in the moonlight. Their red, green, and yellow signals were cheery. "Isn't it beautiful?" Maggie observed.

"What I wish—I wish there was more traffic," Christopher said. "If we were to break down . . ."

Maggie cut him off. "We won't."

"That's the difference between you and me," Christopher said. "I look for the worst to happen, you the best."

"Might as well," she said.

Christopher sniffed. "Do you smell alcohol?"

"I smell onion," Maggie said.

"If she boils dry we're in trouble. She was already overloaded without those books of yours. What do you need with all those books? Why didn't you sell them?"

"You know why," Maggie said. What she had sold was her car—for thirty dollars on the spot when Christopher arrived in town and offered her a ride almost all the way home. The booking of Christopher the Great out of Fort Wayne called a minimum of five performances a week; they were promoted, in the name of the sponsoring local charity, by five women, each working a town a week in advance of Christopher, and moving on the day after the performance. There were towns like Glens Falls, N.Y.; Oil Town, Pa.; Pittsfield, Mass.; and Bluefield that Maggie wasn't ever going to forget.

Christopher took off his mitten and groped for her hand where it was snuggled in her pocket. "I love you, Maggie, books and all. I love you the best of all my girls."

"I love you, too," she lied—or half lied—and gave her hand to keep him from groping any farther.

The road soon demanded both his hands on the steering wheel. He started to sing, "You tell me your dreams, I'll tell you mine . . ."

Maggie sang harmony, a strong alto to his quavering tenor.

They were almost an hour into their journey when a thump, thump, thump signaled a flat tire. Christopher cursed philosophically and pulled to the side of the road. It took all his wirey strength to jack up the overloaded Chevy, a rock wedged under the other rear wheel. While he removed the loosened bolts by moonlight, Maggie went behind a billboard to pee. The billboard featured Santa Claus, a Coca-Cola in his hand: "The pause that keeps you going." Christopher was blowing on his hands. A vast silence surrounded them. Then from inside the car came the cooing of his doves. Maggie laughed.

"It ain't funny, Maggie," the magician said. "They never coo at night."

Then came another sound in the far distance, the fluted whistle of a train. Maggie wished she were on the train, but didn't say so. She needed all her money to buy a few family Christmas presents and a warmer coat. If she had told her dream it was that she could get a job teaching history. She adored history. She was carrying twelve volumes of English history that had belonged to her grandfather, along with several volumes of poetry. An English major, a minor in history, she was overeducated for the jobs available.

A car went by so fast it almost sucked her with it. Christopher shouted curses after it. An echo made them resound. "Helloooooo," Maggie called and her voice bounced around the hills. "Go to hell!" Christopher shouted. Hell, hell, hell, hell . . . A few minutes later he eased the car down, strapped the flat tire into place, and put his tools in the trunk. He went behind the billboard. Maggie warmed her hands on the radiator.

"I should've saved it," he said, returning. "Did I ever tell you about the time in Iron Mountain when the radiator went dry?"

"You did, you did!" One night every week after the show they would find a friendly tavern, drink beer and eat fried fish, French fries, and cole slaw. They'd play the jukebox and dance until the place closed. Christopher told several versions of his life story. She still didn't know his last name unless it was Christopher. In which case she didn't know his first name. One of his stories made her cry the first time she heard it—how he had wanted to be a pianist when he was a kid. His mother stole from the family food allowance to get him lessons and then somehow managed to buy a piano. His father made him play for him one day while he sat beside him on the piano bench. All of a sudden, without any warning, he slammed the lid down on the boy's fingers. Three of them were broken. It was the doctor who got him doing magic tricks to make the fingers nimble again.

Maggie climbed back into the front seat, kicked her heels against her books, and tried to rub warmth into her arms. There was a heater but it leaked engine fumes and Christopher was afraid they might kill his doves or the rabbit.

According to a road sign they were forty miles out of Bluefield. Maggie said she was getting hungry. Christopher offered her a Milky Way. She had given up mushy chocolate in high school.

"How about half an onion?"

"No thank you," Maggie said and started to sing "Stormy Weather," her all-time favorite song.

They had almost made it to the top of a long climb when the car began to chug. The smell of alcohol grew stronger and stronger. Steam was escaping from the radiator. Christopher kept coaxing the hiccoughing car, "Come on, gal, I'm your pal . . ." He managed to pull off the road before the engine gave out. The "sealer" hadn't worked, he said and cursed the garage man who had sold it to him with a money back guarantee—in Bluefield.

They searched the roadside, Maggie on one side, Christopher on the other, for a promising-looking house, then for just any house. There didn't seem to be one. Christopher worried about his props, his twenty thousand dollars' worth of equipment, more or less, a priceless white rabbit, and a pair of turtledoves.

Below them and running roughly parallel to the road was the railway track, even more sparsely traveled than the highway. Christopher was carrying a two-gallon milk can he hoped to fill with water. He waved it overhead and shouted as a pickup truck went by. It didn't stop.

A metallic glow appeared ahead, illusive at first as a will-o'-the-wisp. It turned out to be a mailbox. They followed the rutted road that wended downhill from it. The road soon divided and still they could see no buildings. But from where they then stood they saw a railroad crossing and the crossing guard's house. The light in it was like a beacon of civilization. Christopher figured that it had to be where the highway they were on crossed the tracks. If they could get the Chevy to the top of the hill they could coast all the way down. A raucous shriek shattered the stillness. It hit Maggie like a bolt of pain.

"It's a goddamn jackass," Christopher said. And to prove itself the animal gave several long hee-haws. That started a dog barking nearby. "Let's get the hell back to the car," Christopher said.

He talked to the car and patted the radiator before getting in.

"I'm praying," Maggie said when he put his foot on the starter.

"Can't hurt."

The motor turned over, sputtered between life and death, took more gas, and when Christopher shot the car into gear it leaped ahead. Alongside the mailbox it began to chug again. "You can make it, baby. I know you can." When it was on the verge of conking out, he threw it out of gear, revved the motor, and thrust it into gear again. It leaped a few yards more. They made it, cheering, to the top and began the long, winding descent. "Now you better pray we can stop," he said.

The first thing Christopher noticed when they pulled off the road a few feet their side of the tracks was a well pump, a cup hanging on a chain alongside. The light in the crossing guard's house seemed dimmer close up than it had at a distance. In fact, there was no window this side, what they were seeing was reflected light. "You go in and ask him if we can get warm and have some water," the magician ordered. "But just in case he's ornery, I'm going to fill her up right now." He left the engine running and took off his scarf to muzzle the steam when he removed the radiator cap.

Maggie approached the little house through the stubble of a railside garden. The guard's STOP sign hung beside the door. She wondered why women couldn't be railway guards: all that time to read and a cozy rabbit hutch of a house. She rapped on the door and observed in the reflected light trackside that there was also a coal bin there. No one answered her knock. Sleep, she decided, must be a terrible temptation. Christopher was pumping. No water yet. The pump sounded a little like the donkey. She knocked again and thought of the poem, "The Listeners."

"Eureka!" Christopher cried and she heard the splash of water.

She did not like to try the door. The guard might be doing God knew what. She went around to the window. It was bleary with dust. A halo surrounded a naked light bulb hanging from the ceiling. She rapped on the glass and cleared a place to look in. A gray-haired man was slumped in a rocker, his legs sprawled toward the stove, his back to the door. His chin was on his breast and a newspaper lay on the floor at the side of his chair. A fire glowed in the potbellied stove. She rapped again on the window, this time with her class ring. He made no move. She ran back to where Christopher was lugging the can of water.

"There's something wrong with the old man in there. I think maybe he's dead."

"Dead asleep," he said. "Get in the car."

"We can't just drive off and leave him."

"Why not? That's what people have been doing to us all night," Christopher shouted, pulling back from a burst of steam. "I'm going to get another can of water and move on."

"Chris, I'm going back and see what's wrong with him."

"What do you think you are, a doctor? And don't call me Chris."

Maggie ran back to the house. This time she opened the door. The big railway clock over the desk said 3:10. Every tick sounded as though it was going to be the last. The old man was in the same position as he was when she'd seen him from the window. "Mister . . ." She approached him tentatively and touched his hand. It was terribly cold although the room was warm.

Christopher came in muttering about putting a beggar on horseback. "Holy Christ," he then said reverently. He walked slowly around the chair, stepping carefully over the old man's feet. He stopped and pointed a trembling finger to where a thin trickle of blood dribbled from the man's ear onto his shoulder. "That means he was hit in the back of the head. Have you got a mirror?"

"In the car," she said. "Should I go get it?"

"Never mind." Christopher went to the desk and picked up the phone. It was dead. He hung up and tried it again. Quite dead. A telegraph signal began to rap out of the apparatus on the desk. They just looked at one another. Neither of them understood Morse code, but the staccato transmission made the message sound urgent.

"If there's a train coming through we can flag it down," Maggie said.

"Like we did the cars," Christopher said.

"Look, this can't have happened long ago. If we saw the light from way up there it had to be through the open door, right?" She hurried outdoors in time to see a change in the colored signals alongside the northbound track, green off, yellow on. The train gave a long series of whistles and the automatic warning lights began to blink at the roadway crossing, the bell to ring furiously although there was not a

113

car in sight. Maggie caught up the guard's sign from alongside the door. The great white eye appeared from the south; clouds of steam billowed up and fell back over the engine to shroud the cars behind. The track signal switched from yellow back to green. For just an instant Maggie caught sight of an automobile parked on the other side of the northbound track. The oncoming engine blocked it out. Then, a man jumped out of the darkness nearly opposite to where she had seen the car. He stood on the southbound track and waved at the oncoming train. Someone in the cab threw a sack down to him. Maggie lost sight of him in a billow of smoke.

"Christopher?" She called out as though he might do something.

He was right behind her. "No!"

The engine came abreast of them. Maggie waved the sign and shouted, "Man dead, man dead!" and pointed at the house.

The trainman waved at her, but heard nothing, she was sure, what with the grind of the wheels, the warning whistle, and the accelerating *chu-chu-chu-chu—chu-chu-chu-chu* . . . The train plowed on leaving them, too, in a spray of smoke.

She turned her back to the smoke and saw the man again, running toward the rear of the train; he had to get around it to get to the car. She started after him. Christopher brought her down with a flying tackle. Struggling to get up she saw the lights go on in the car on the other side of the train. "They'll get away," she shouted.

"You're damn right they will!" Christopher headed for the Chevy.

Maggie took a last look down the tracks. Now the man was running toward her alongside the train. A few yards before he reached her he jumped for the ladder on the side of a boxcar, caught it, and swung himself onto the steps. For just an instant she thought of trying to grab hold of him but he was too soon past. The train picked up speed. Between the passing boxcars she saw the other automobile drive along the tracks as far as the road and then turn north. She caught sight of the man with the packet in the light of the crossing. He was clinging like a barnacle to the side of the boxcar.

Maggie looked into the flagman's house from the door. He seemed more dead, as if that were possible, and she didn't even know the telegraph code for S.O.S. She galloped back to Christopher's car and clambered in. The caboose was rolling by.

"You kicked me in the teeth," Christopher said. "I think you've ruined my needle act."

"Sorry," she said, although she wasn't. The needle act was disgusting. "Christopher, could we try and catch up with that other car and see where it goes?"

"What about getting help for that poor old man back there?" Pure sarcasm.

"We can send it. And if he's dead, he's dead, isn't he?"

A snowball had a better chance in hell than they had of catching the other car, so Christopher said he'd try.

Maggie studied the road map under the flashlight. "You know what? We'll be coming into Williamson soon. I'll bet the train stops there and that's where they'll meet up. I'll bet I'm right."

"And what if you are? What do we do then?"

"I wish we had a gun," she said.

"What?"

"I told you once, my father's a deputy sheriff. He's a farmer, but he's also a deputy sheriff."

"I don't like guns and I don't like deputy sheriffs," Christopher said. "Process servers, that's all they are."

"All the same," Maggie said. Then: "I'll bet that was a mailbag they snatched. The way he waved his arms—that could be how the old man did it every night."

"Okay, tell me something if you're so smart," the magician said. "Why bump the old guy off first? Why not grab the mailbag from him after the train's gone through and nobody's around? If it was a mailbag."

"Because . . ." Maggie said slowly, "they didn't mean to kill him. He was asleep and they just wanted to make sure he stayed that way and didn't see who they were. I'll bet they live around here. It's Christmas and they're broke. There was bound to be money in the mail. Christopher, can't we go any faster?"

"You make me nervous every time you say Christopher. We got about five miles left before she boils dry again."

"There could be a reward, you know, and we'd split it," Maggie said. "Hey! Where's your stage gun, the one you shoot the rabbit with?" It was another of his tricks that Maggie didn't like. She was pretty sure he had a deaf rabbit because of it.

"It's in the green metal box with the silks," he said. "Just don't upset the goddamn livestock."

Maggie, her knees on the seat, flashlight in hand, began the search for the green box. A car passed, going the opposite direction.

"That's your guy going back to pick up his buddy on the tracks."

"No," Maggie said. Through a small space between boxes she saw the train running parallel to them, sometimes quite close. She prayed they wouldn't have to cross the tracks again before Williamson. They'd never make it to the crossing first. She also prayed she could find the green box. She shone the flashlight into the sad, pink eyes of the rabbit where he stared

116

out the window of his case.

"Williamson's a ghost town since the Depression," Christopher said. "The train won't stop there."

"Want to bet?" She spotted the green metal box on the floor. It was underneath three suitcases and the Chinese Head Chopper. She had to change places with the rabbit to get to it. Talk about Alice in Wonderland. It took a long time but she got the box out. By then her fingers were numb.

"Williamson, three miles," Christopher read a road sign.

"Any sign of their car?"

"I can see a taillight if that's what you mean."

"It's theirs," she said with conviction, changing places again with the rabbit. She got out the gun and four blank cartridges, wedged the box between the rabbit and the cage of turtledoves, and loaded a cartridge. That was all the starter's pistol would take at a time.

"I must be crazy to give you that," Christopher said. "What do you think you're going to do with it?"

"Just have it."

They were losing ground to the train, running even at the moment with the caboose.

"Try and keep up, Christopher. Maybe I'll catch sight of him."

Christopher swore at damn-fool women who thought they were Annie Oakleys.

Williamson *was* a ghost town, to judge by the outskirts. The streetlights were dead—empty, broken globes. Houses were boarded up. Even the billboards were bare. But the train was slowing down, its whistle sharp and measured, a distinct signal. A trainman came out onto the caboose platform and began to work what seemed to be levers. A noisy shudder ran the length of the train.

"It's stopping," Maggie said, and they were passing car after car now. Between two of the cars she glimpsed a figure with a great hump on his back. "I see him!" she cried. "I'll bet he jumps before they stop."

"He'll kill himself if he does. He must be frozen stiff."

Suddenly they lost complete sight of the train where the road made a hairpin turn, going steeply downhill. When they saw it again it was dead ahead, stopped across the tracks.

A thin row of high-slung lights lined the station platform. Light shone from the stationmaster's office, but the rest of what once was an elegant gabled building was in spooky darkness. The car Maggie convinced herself they had followed was parked next to the platform. Christopher wouldn't drive near it.

"Okay, park and we'll walk," Maggie said. "Just pretend we're going to report the old man to the stationmaster."

"I'm not pretending. That's all I am going to do." He turned the Chevy around and parked facing the highway which continued parallel to the tracks. Main Street crossed the tracks down into the town. "If anything happens run like hell back here. They'll find that old man without us."

Maggie trudged to the platform, passing close to the parked car. She didn't go right up to look but she couldn't see anyone in it. Maybe it wasn't their car at all. The train let out an enormous sigh, every car simultaneously. Down the platform, on the other side of the office a man in a railway cap and a sheepskin coat was handing up bags from a Railway Express wagon. Behind Maggie the crossing bell was clanging furiously as though it could waken a dead town. More than half the train stretched out of sight beyond the Main Street crossing.

She looked around to see where Christopher was. He had cut over in front of the parked car and was striding along the platform toward where the baggage was being loaded. She'd be willing to bet he wouldn't even mention the man they'd seen jumping the train. She ran to catch up with him but cast a glance over her shoulder every few steps. The magician and the stationmaster were talking when she looked back and saw two men running alongside the tracks, their figures caught for the moment in the crossing light. They were headed for the parked car.

She shouted, "Christopher!" He paid no attention. She ran back. The men separated, one on a beeline to the car and the other headed, stiff-legged, for the highway. No, she realized, he was heading for Christopher's car. She dug the pistol out of her pocket and fired its single shot. A pop. A mere pop. Another cartridge might be louder but she was too shaken to reload. Her heart felt like it was beating itself to death, but she ran full speed for the Chevrolet. The other car roared into motion behind her. Its lights circled her: the driver meant to run her down or scare her off the road. She flung herself toward the bushes and kept rolling over and over. By the time she was safe and recovered her senses, both cars were heading onto the highway and on back the way they'd come. Christopher was running from the station, shouting "Stop! You thieving bastards, stop!"

Maggie picked herself up and made it to where the magician was sobbing with rage.

"He almost ran me over," Maggie said.

"They've got my rabbit! They've got my whole goddamn life! What have you done to me, Maggie?"

She didn't say anything until the lights of both cars disappeared. Then her mind began to work again. "What do they want with your car anyway? They won't take it far. All they want is a head start so we can't follow them again. Come on, Chris," she coaxed. "Take one more chance on me. Let's hike as far as the turn in the road." She hooked her arm through his and pulled him forward.

"Don't call me Chris," he muttered.

As they neared the turn, the whole valley below them seemed swathed in a shimmering mist, a few pinpricks of light showing through. It was like an upside-down sky. "Isn't it beautiful?" Maggie exclaimed.

"Shut up," Christopher said.

But when they rounded the curve he cried out, "By God, you're right! There she is!"

The Chevy sat in stubborn majesty, her radiator against the guardrail of the overlook.

Christopher turned the car around and refilled the radiator from the milk can. Maggie got in and thought about how long it had been since she'd got out of bed the previous morning. She had pawned her watch in Danbury, Connecticut, in October and lost the ticket in Framingham, Massachusetts, but she had a Baby Ben alarm clock in her book bag. She reached for it and knew at once that what was at her feet was not her book bag.

She sat very still and didn't say a word until they were about to pass the Williamson station. "Christopher, you'd better stop."

"No, ma'am," he said.

"My book bag is gone. They've taken it."

"Hurray for them."

She pulled the bag at her feet up onto her lap.

"What's that?" he said, and then, "Oh, my God."

He slammed on the brakes and even by what was left of the moonlight they could read the marking, U.S. MAIL.

"I reckon we'll get your books back for you, ma'am," the sheriff of Mingo County said, "but I can't guarantee it'll be by noon." Noontime was the hour at which the best garage repairman in Tug River Valley had promised a mended radiator and two new tires. The sheriff figured that in due time the Norfolk and Western Railway might just pay for them. "But you'll be yonder by a long ways then."

The magician and Maggie had had a few hours' sleep at opposite ends of an old leather sofa in the sheriff's office. His wife had brought them a wonderful breakfast of ham, fried cornmeal mush, and eggs, with coffee enough to keep them awake all the way to the Michigan state line. The rabbit nibbled carrots from the woman's root cellar, the doves traveled with their own supply of birdseed. Christopher took a five-dollar gold piece out of the sheriff's wife's ear and put it in her apron pocket—to give her kids for Christmas.

"I knew when I heard your story," the sheriff summed things up, "it had to be the McCoy brothers. They weren't ever known to do anything the easy way if they could find a hard one. And folks got to thank the good Lord that most times they're just plain unlucky. Like your turning up tonight. A couple of years back they aimed to rob the local bank. They squeezed themselves through the ventilating system during the night and was inside waiting for the manager to open up the next morning. Only trouble, that was the day President Roosevelt closed every bank in the country. Nobody opened up. Some people round here blamed it on the McCoys at first. Dang near lynched them. They'd've saved us a pack of trouble since if they had."

The sheriff took off his hat, scratched his head, and put his hat back on again. "It may turn out the best luck they ever did have was you finding the old man. They could hang for that if he don't pull through. But that old man is tougher than all the McCoys put together. It won't surprise me none if he lives to be state's witness."

Maggie and Christopher looked at one another. Then Maggie asked the question: "What's the old man's name, Sheriff?"

"Smith. Just plain Willie Smith."

The Scream

Sally had called him a "mother's boy" when he wanted to leave the party at eleven. It hurt and angered him, but what angered him most was that he hadn't left right then. He stayed on as though that was going to change her feelings toward him. She'd turned her attention to guys he didn't even know and didn't think she did. She said she'd hitch a ride in one of the other cars. Now he was really late. He drove up the ravine trail furiously, scattering stones and gravel, ripping through the bramble. Midnight wasn't late for that gang, even on a school night, even though they'd lost the beer to the cops who had intercepted them on the way down. He had an old-fashioned mother who pretended she wasn't a single parent. Sometimes she told people her husband was away on business. But sometimes, when she and David were alone, she would call him the man of the house and say how much she depended on him.

As soon as he cleared the park drive he opened up the Chevy. He'd got in the habit of worrying about his mother when he didn't get home on time. This angered him, too. What he worried about was her worrying about him, and it made him feel tied up. Or down. He kept flooring the accelerator until he turned off the highway onto a two-way shortcut via the old County Road.

He thought of Sally and the guy who'd been trying to make out with her when David took off. He was a wimp. David hated him. Sally seemed to like wimps. She had an overload of energy and breasts like ice cream cones. He hit top speed again. Nobody used the County Road except the locals. With not a car in sight, he reached into his breast pocket and fished out the orange packet. He rolled down the window thinking, One more for the road: his joke on himself. He had yet to use one of the damn things in a real situation, yet to suggest to Sally or any other woman that he had one in his pocket. He threw it out against the wind and felt immediately that it might have blown back into the car. He glanced around. In less than a breath of time he turned back to the road. A car, dead ahead, no lights, had stopped half on the pavement, half on the shoulder. He swerved across the middle line, then starting to careen, he let the wheel take control. The Chevy swung back and he saw the woman coming around in front of the parked car. He saw her scream. Didn't hear it. Her face, the mouth wide, seemed to zoom at him. He pulled the car away from her and fought to control it by acceleration. The woman flung herself against her car, sandwiched between it and the Chevy when he passed. He got command, his hands frozen around the steering wheel. He was faint with fear, but he hadn't hit her. He was sure of it. He would have heard something, a thump, a noise, something, if he had. He was sure of it. He did not stop.

"Davie, is that you? Are you just getting in?"

"I've been downstairs for a while," he lied. He squeezed the words through a dry, tight throat.

"Then you should have finished your studies before you went out."

"I know." At her bedroom door he said, "Good night, Mother."

"I need a kiss," she said, and when he brushed her forehead with his lips, "Now I'll be able to sleep."

He drew the door almost closed. The cat wriggled through and followed him down the hall. It wove itself between his legs in the bathroom and then rubbed against him when he sat on the edge of his bed to take off his sneakers. As soon as he removed one, the cat jumped it and worried its head into the toe.

"Allie, it stinks!" He buried his face in the crook of his arm. "Like me."

He woke up before he finished the Our Father. In the next second the spiraling plane would have hit the ground. He lay, abruptly wide awake, knowing what he had dreamt, and wondered why he had not been scared. He'd felt calm and oblivious to the other passengers, who were also about to die. "Forgive us our trespasses . . ." Suddenly he remembered the face he'd kept seeing while he lay in bed last night, unable to fall asleep, the scream he couldn't hear. If he looked at the wall now he would see it again. If he closed his eyes he would see it. He wrenched himself out of bed. Every bone in his body ached. Every muscle was taut.

His mother called to him from downstairs wanting to know if he was up. She had called him before and he had fallen back into sleep, into the dream. He leaned over the banister and shouted down that he'd be ready in ten minutes. In the shower he told himself that he must go back to where it happened. What good would it do now? He couldn't have hurt her. She'd have been scared, fainted maybe. But how could he *not* have hurt her? With him going at that speed, the wind could have pulled her to him. But he'd have known it, felt it. And if he had, wouldn't he have stopped? He had not stopped. That was why he had to go back.

David resembled his mother. He was slight, with straight, tawny hair, very blue eyes. The sharp, delicate features made him feel that he looked like a choirboy. He'd got in the habit of pulling down the corners of his mouth. Tough guy, his mother said of it once, which was exactly what he wanted. The one thing he didn't want now was his mother getting a good look at his bloodshot eyes. "I had an awful dream before I woke up," he said. It might explain or distract.

She sat, her chin in her hand, and watched him pour milk shakily into his cornflakes, not seeming to notice anything different in him from other mornings. She was dressed for work, waiting for her ride to arrive any minute. "Want to sort it out?" she said.

"I was going down in a plane crash. There were lots of people screaming, but I wasn't scared." He'd made up the screaming part. He couldn't remember them screaming.

"What else do you remember? Little things," she coaxed. She liked to interpret his dreams for him. She had done it since he was a little kid, a game he kind of liked.

Now he wished he hadn't mentioned this one. "I woke up before we crashed."

"If you weren't scared, what were your feelings?"

He shrugged. "Like philosophical. I said the Our Father." He pushed away from the table. "Mom, I got to go. Professor Joseph always calls first on the kids who come in at the last minute. We call him Sneaky Joe."

"You miss your father. That's what your dream's about."

"Yeah." He got up. The cornflakes barely touched, he put the dish on the floor for the cat.

"Why don't you write and tell him that, Davie?"

Again he shrugged.

"I know you could tell him things you don't tell me," his mother said.

"Okay, Mom, I'll do that." He was desperate to get away from her. He couldn't even manage the usual peck on the cheek.

"Are you going to be all right to drive?" she called after him.

"Why not?" Each day he drove the twenty miles to St. Mary's College, picking up two classmates on the way.

"You're jittery. You're working too hard. You ought not to work late at night. Your sleep's important, Davie. You're still growing."

"Yes, Mother. Yes!" If only her ride would come. He wanted to call his passengers and tell them they had to get to school on their own that morning. It would commit him to going back there.

She called after him: "I have pot roast in the Crock-Pot if you'd like to bring someone home to dinner."

He was shocked at the scratches on the fender and the door when he first saw the car in daylight. It must have happened going down or coming up from the water's edge. Going down he'd been concentrating on Sally's hand getting nearer and nearer his thigh. And then the Sheriff's Patrol had stopped the three cars and confiscated the beer. The cops had made them get out of the cars, and they asked each one if they had any joints or other dope. They hadn't searched anybody. Sally said afterward that if the deputy had laid a finger on her, her father would have had his badge by morning. Some of the other boys went to St. Mary's too, which had turned coeducational recently. Like him they were day students, but they were upperclassmen. One of the deputies had flashed his torch in David's face and then asked to see his driver's license. He couldn't believe David was a college student. Sally tittered. She didn't say it then, but later—mother's boy. He took a chamois to the scratches and turned up the local station on the radio. The only traffic incident reported was a three-car crash on the interstate. He'd bet no one ran away from that one.

The macadam was still silvery from the overnight frost when he turned onto County Road. Tire tracks crisscrossed and then disappeared where the sun's first rays skimmed the surface. The temptation to turn back was getting to him. He made himself go on, one road sign to the next. He reached the underpass beneath the suburban railway. Then he lost his nerve. He turned around beneath the arch and headed for school.

It was too late to go to his first class. In the library he asked at the desk if he could see the *County Sentinel*, not yet on the shelf. The librarian wanted to know if he had a hot number. The lottery. "Look, you never know," David said.

He went through the paper column by column. "Crime Watch": "The Sheriff's Patrol reported no arrests, significant crimes or serious accidents." He was disappointed. Crazy, but that was how he felt. He returned the paper and headed for his second class. It struck him then: the accident on the interstate had not been reported either. It was too soon. But not for it to have been on the radio. Could that mean that nothing very serious had happened on County Road? But something had happened. Suppose he never found out. He didn't think he'd forget it. But say that woman wasn't supposed to be where she was, it was a stolen car maybe, and say that by a miracle she wasn't hurt, or suppose there was someone in the car she wasn't supposed to be with, say someone dragged her into the car afterward. Maybe she *was* hurt. Or dead. If she had banged her head, say, on her own car, he wouldn't have heard that, would he? Just because he hadn't heard anything didn't mean nothing happened. All morning he kept turning over in his mind different possibilities, knowing that only one of them, or maybe none, was so. His imagination would not let go. He was such a good liar, why couldn't he lie to himself? He ought to keep track of the lies he told. A priest once said to him about confession, "Don't simply pick a number as though it's a lottery." Which was exactly what he used to do.

Lying was his big problem from when he was a little kid. It always surprised him that people, his mother for example, took for granted he was telling the truth. Or did they pretend, too? Pretend they believed him. During his first session with the St. Mary's student advisor they'd had a long talk on why people lied, even professional liars like spies, and what it did to a man's character to lie habitually. Women did it for fun, the advisor said, and then added quickly that he was making a joke. David wasn't sure. But he wound up taking as his elective the Christian Ethics course the advisor recommended. His mother was pleased. Someone told her Father Moran would be supportive. Of a student with a father absent from home David supposed, though nobody said it to him.

He kept making up excuses to himself to skip ethics class that afternoon. He didn't want to blurt out something he couldn't explain. The kids taking the class were hound dogs on the scent for heresy. Some of them had flunked out of seminary and were going through a kind of rehab. Father Moran paid them special attention. The Church needed more priests and nuns to make up for the dropouts. Father Moran was one of the few religious on the faculty and probably wouldn't have lasted at St. Mary's till now if there wasn't the shortage.

David kept returning to his car all morning to catch the local news on the radio. He was nauseous, and in the mirror he looked as pale as a boiled potato. In the mirror, behind his own face, was the image of a man approaching, looking, David thought, at the license numbers of the cars as he worked his way through the parking lot. David felt in his bones the man was looking for him. He switched off the radio.

The stranger wore an out-of-date polo coat that was too

big for him and a slouch hat that made his face look small, his features pinched, mean. He stooped to look in at David and took a quick survey of the inside of the car at the same time. He pushed his hat back and gestured that he wanted David to roll his window down. Reluctantly David obliged.

The man couldn't smile. The attempt was like a nervous tic. "You're David Crowley, right? I'm Dennis McGraw." He handed David his business card:

DENNIS HENRY MCGRAW

ATTORNEY-AT-LAW

"I'm an associate of Deputy Sheriff Addy Muller's. Deputy Muller was on the welcoming committee when you and your friends went down to the beach last night." He gave the tic of a smile. "He could have hauled you in—you know, a public beach. Do you mind if I get in the car with you? It's cold out here."

"I have a class in twenty minutes, Mr. McGraw."

But the man was already lurching around to the passenger side. He took notice of the scratches and pursed his lips to show his awareness. He eased into the seat alongside David. His coat overflowed it. "They say it's going to rain. Feels more like snow. It's a funny time of year for a beach party. Coming up Halloween, I suppose. And privacy's no problem on the beach in October, is it?" Again, the smirk. "Relax, David. We'll get you to your class on time. Addy said it was a long shot, but he remembered you lived in Oak Forest and could have been driving on the County Road last night. . . ."

Once again the lie seemed safer to David. He shook his head.

"The interstate?"

"That's right," David said.

"Well, Addy said it was a long shot. I don't know why anyone would take the County Road unless the interstate was shut down . . . or they had some mischief in mind. About what time was it when you got home?"

David took alarm. He ought not to have lied. He pumped himself up and said, "It's none of your business, mister, and if you don't get out of this car, I'm going to turn you over to the security police."

McGraw spread his hands. "What did I say?"

"I want to know why you're asking me these questions."

"You aren't giving me a chance to tell you."

If David could have stopped his ears, he would have, rather than hear the very thing he wanted to know.

"But there's no point to it if you didn't take the County Road," McGraw went on. "The reason I asked about the time: there was an accident that shut down the interstate for a couple of hours after midnight. Nobody got through going your direction."

David was about to say that he must have got through just ahead, but he bit his tongue. He might be able to back out now before he got in deeper. "Could I see your identification, Mr. McGraw? Anybody could pick up that business card you showed me."

"Smart boy. I'm like Abe Lincoln, David. I have an office but mostly I carry my business in my hat. All you got to do is call up the Sheriff's Office and speak to Deputy Addy Muller. He'll tell you who I am."

David drew a deep breath, and tried to lie himself out of the lie. "I didn't want to get involved in anything. I mean you're a lawyer and that generally means trouble."

"I can't argue with you on that, David. I'm the first person my clients call when they get in trouble."

"I did go home by the County Road, but I don't know what time it was. I was supposed to be in by midnight."

"Driving alone, were you?"

"I didn't know many kids at the party. My girlfriend invited me."

"Didn't you take the young lady home?"

"She got a ride from one of the other guys. I don't know what you want from me, but I've got to go now and I want to lock the car."

"Five minutes more?" McGraw said.

"No, sir. I don't know you and I don't see why I should talk to you."

"Then I'll tell you what you should do, David. First chance, drive over to the Sheriff's Office. You know where that is. Ask for Deputy Muller. He's investigating an incident on the County Road last night. He's looking for witnesses."

And there it was: something *had* happened. He'd run away from something real. "Okay, I'll do that," David muttered, his voice shaky. Then, realizing what hadn't been said: "Witness to what?"

"If you don't know, you better ask Deputy Muller." McGraw stuck out his hand as though expecting David to shake it. He withdrew it before David had a chance to take or refuse it. "Unless you'd like me to represent you? I'm well thought of in the County Building. It's never a mistake to have legal counsel, David, always a mistake to go it on your own. You told me you went home on the interstate. Why did you tell that little lie? Addy's going to want to know."

David turned the key in the ignition. He wasn't sure what to do—one security guard for the whole campus. He had to get rid of this guy. He was a crook, an ambulance chaser. But he knew something.

"No hard feelings," McGraw said. He opened the car door

and slipped out, pulling his coat after him. It clung to the seat and he had to yank it free. David wanted to laugh. And cry. McGraw stood wriggling, trying to straighten himself inside the oversize garment. David revved the motor and circled fast. There was a terrible familiarity to the whirr of the tires. He did not look back.

The whole class jumped on him when he said he thought Judas Iscariot wasn't as bad as the Christians made him out to be. Maybe he thought of himself as a whistle-blower, that Jesus wasn't good for the Jewish people—"Too much forgiveness—you know, like the woman who committed adultery."

"Money, money, money," students in the back of the room chanted. "He did it for money." It was their way of breaking into David's tirade.

"But he didn't want the money. Look what he did with it!" David didn't know what was happening to him to be shooting off like this. He didn't even know how long he'd been on his feet. Father Moran had settled his backside on the edge of the desk and folded his arms like a fat Buddha. He was enjoying himself. He loved it when his boys got their adrenaline flowing. Always his boys—he hadn't yet got used to the presence of girls in the class. "I don't think Jesus himself was fair to him," David went on. "He knew Judas was in trouble. He was the one who said the disciples should pray 'Lead us not into temptation.' Man, did Judas ever get led into temptation. What I'm saying is, Jesus knew. He knew what was going to happen to Judas. Look what he said to Saint Peter: 'Before the cock crows, you'll deny me three times.' And Peter did. And he cried. So did Judas. He went out and wept bitterly." David lost his train of thought. Actually, it was Peter who went out and wept bitterly.

Father Moran took over. "Well, Crowley. You certainly got our adrenaline flowing. Watch out the devil doesn't catch up with you. He's always on the lookout for a good advocate." The priest shifted his weight, one buttock to the other. "Tell me, what do you understand to be Iscariot's greater sin—that he betrayed the Lord or that he despaired of being forgiven?"

"Despair is the greatest sin." It was an answer out of his childhood catechism.

"Why?"

"I don't know, Father." He did not want to be quizzed like a ten-year-old. His moment of self-assurance was going down the drain.

The priest nodded to one of the volunteers. The back row all had their hands up.

Then David caught hold of another idea. "But despair is a sin against yourself, isn't it? Being your own judge. Betraying somebody is worse, it seems to me. You're hurting somebody else."

"Mitchell, you're on," the priest said to the volunteer, ignoring David's attempted postscript, except to say, "Thank you, Crowley."

David tried to listen to Mitchell's definition of despair as a sin against hope, and his denunciation of Judas because he had given up hope. It went on and on. David could have put it in one sentence. Somebody had done that, he realized, which was how it came into his mind: Abandon hope, all ye who enter here. Meaning hell.

It looked like the class wasn't going to get back on track until everybody had their say on why Judas was so despicable—the kiss, the pieces of silver; somebody said he was jealous of John, the disciple whom Jesus loved. "I know! He was gay!" one of the girls put in. She covered her mouth and giggled. The giggle was infectious and those around her laughed. David pretended to be amused, but he wasn't. He felt he'd been on to something important and had been cut off before he got to the heart of it. He'd had a question he wanted to ask that he felt would shake up even Father Moran. Now he couldn't remember it.

Between Christian Ethics and his last class, he copied a friend's notes for Twentieth Century French Literature, the class he had missed that morning, but his mind kept going back to Dennis McGraw and what he called "the incident" the sheriff's deputy was investigating. You wouldn't call anything serious an incident, would you? Suppose he found out tomorrow that the screaming person had not been hurt, not the least bit hurt, that the scream was an act, would that mean he was not guilty of anything? Look now: was guilt a matter of luck? Getting caught was, maybe. Wasn't that why he was in ethics, to learn why getting caught was not part of the moral issue? And wasn't getting caught what he was really afraid of? He didn't care about that woman at all. Not for her own sake. The person he cared about was David Crowley.

He tried to focus on the Valéry poem in which he was supposed to trace the Symbolist influence, but he couldn't concentrate. It was hopeless, and he was supposed to be good in French. David felt as though something inside him was writhing, a stomachful of snakes. The school day was almost over, but terrible as it had been he dreaded for it to end. He didn't want to go home. He had to talk to someone. For just a minute he wondered if he should have been such a smart-ass with Dennis McGraw. McGraw wanted to talk to him. McGraw knew something. He didn't.

On his way home he thought about his father and what his mother had said at breakfast, how he could tell his father things he couldn't tell her. He was pretty sure she was talking about sex, but if his father was around would he be able to tell him what he'd done, how he'd run away when he might have hurt somebody? He could see his father going out to the car and saying, "Get in, David." He'd order David's mother back into the house and he'd drive straight to the Sheriff's Office and say, "My son has a statement to make." Even so, David thought, he could tell him sooner than he could tell his mother. What he wanted most was not to have to tell anybody, to wake up and find out it was a dream.

He drove around the block twice before turning into the driveway in case McGraw or someone from the Sheriff's Office was waiting for him. He saw no one, and when he parked in front of the garage door, the nearest neighbor was coming out of her house. She waved to him, got into her car, and drove off. Perfectly normal. In the house he got the same feeling of normalcy. It made him uneasy, as if he might step where there was nothing for his foot to land on. There were no messages for him on the answering machine. Even the cat ignored him. He looked up Dennis McGraw in the yellow pages. He'd thought he might not be there, but he was, the address the County Building. Something was real, anyway, Dennis McGraw, attorney-at-law. He had an enemy, David thought. For the first time in his life he had a real enemy. That was crazy. All McGraw wanted was to make a buck out of him. *Unless you'd like me to represent you . . .* But David hadn't admitted anything, except going home on the County Road. McGraw had looked for him because Deputy Muller had a hunch. Oughtn't car license numbers to be available to the police only? Everybody knew the Sheriff's Office was corrupt. The patrol shouldn't have just taken the beer away last night, they ought to have chased the kids out of the park or arrested them for bringing beer there in the first place. He wondered if any of the other guys had been approached by McGraw. Whoever took Sally home would have had to use the interstate or the County Road; he hadn't thought of that before. They almost certainly had to go that way, and if they had, it would have been after David's trip home.

He hated to call Sally. He was shaky, and if there was anyone he wanted less than his mother to know what he'd done, it was Sally. He kept putting off calling her until it was almost time for his mother to come home, and then he went out and used the nearest public phone.

"I wanted to be sure you got home all right last night," he explained.

"You'd have known by now if I didn't. It was real mean of you, David, to go and leave me with that pack of wolves."

"I didn't leave you! You said . . . whatever you said. It doesn't matter. What happened?"

"What almost happened on the way home was worse. We had to go the County Road—the interstate was closed. . . ."

"I know," David said. "What happened to *you*, I mean?"

"The guys were fooling around. They're sex fiends, and all of a sudden we almost hit a car parked halfway on the highway. No lights, nobody around, like it died and somebody just left it there."

David saw the whole thing in his mind's eye. "Did you stop?"

"Why should we have? We didn't hit it or anything. But it cooled off Micky's sex urge. When we got to Oak Forest, he dropped me at our driveway and took off."

If the car was still there later, what did it mean? What had happened to the woman?

"If I didn't see it," David said, the words of denial slipping out, "you must have come home a lot later than me."

"Not much. I kind of agitated to get us on the road. I'm sorry I said what I did, David. You shouldn't be so sensitive. Women can be frustrated too, you know. You're not crude like those other guys, and I admire that. I admire a lot about you."

"Thanks," he murmured.

"What do I have to do to make up for what I said? Ask you for another date? I was the one asked you last night, you know."

"I'll call you real soon, Sally."

"I go back to school on Sunday." She was on midterm break.

"I'll call you," he said again.

"Okay, David. Thanks for calling." The phone clicked off.

Now he had hurt her, but he couldn't help it. He stood in the booth after hanging up, and tried to find the words with which he could tell Sally what had happened to him. It went fine until he had to say, I didn't stop. They hadn't stopped either, but they'd not seen the screaming woman.

A man waiting to use the phone pushed open the door. "Do you always go into a phone booth when you want to talk to yourself?"

After an early dinner at the kitchen table David attacked his class assignments. He surprised himself with what sounded to him like a great exposition of the Valéry poem. It felt good, as though he'd made some kind of reparation in getting it done. He took it in to where his mother was writing letters and read it to her. He'd been pretty quiet at dinner and she hadn't fussed or probed. He was making up.

She listened thoughtfully. Then, out of a clear sky, she said, "Would you like a year of study in France if it could be managed?"

David was stunned. It was as though she had said she no longer needed him. He'd been thinking all along that he was tied to her for life, and now it turned out she felt she was tied down by him. Maybe she had a man he didn't even know about, somebody at the bank. . . . A tumult of alarms possessed him.

"Well?" she prompted.

"Yeah, sure. I mean that's a third-year alternative and I'm only a freshman."

"Only a freshman," she repeated. "You put yourself down, Davie. You shouldn't do that. The essay is very good."

"It isn't long enough to call it an essay."

"Nevertheless, would you like to read me the poem itself?"

He was on his way to get the book when the phone rang. His mother called out to let the machine take it for now. He pretended not to hear her. All evening, except for when he lost himself in the poem, he had anticipated something heavy about to happen. Nevertheless, when he heard McGraw's voice, his heart gave a sickening thump.

"David, I hope I'm not interrupting your dinner. We need to make a date, you and I. Tonight is convenient for me, or first thing in the morning."

"No," David said. "It's not convenient for me."

"Then you must make it convenient. It's not a matter of choice, young man. Are you with someone now so that you can't talk?"

"My mother's home," David muttered.

"Well now, sooner or later, you will want to involve her. Maybe not. That's not my business. Let's meet somewhere in the morning. I would say my office, but it's being decorated. Unavailable really. And I don't want to meet in your car again. We're not conspiring thieves, are we?"

"David?" his mother called inquiringly from the study.

"I'll be in in a minute, Mother." To McGraw, he said, "You can come here in the morning, but not before eight-thirty." It was his mother's turn to drive. She'd leave by eight o'clock.

McGraw repeated the time and checked David's address. He had it right.

Returning, book in hand, to where his mother was waiting, David explained, "I got some scratches on my car going down to the beach last night. A guy's going to paint them for me."

"Have it done by a professional, David. I'll help you pay for it."

"Great," he said.

"Not everything is great," she said. Then, "Shall we put off the poem until another time?"

McGraw arrived not long after the hall clock struck the hour. David had again cut loose his riders. He took the lawyer to the kitchen. McGraw was wearing the same topcoat. He took it off and put it on the back of a chair and perched the hat on top of it. "It's a good thing I make house calls, isn't it? Any coffee left in the pot?"

David poured half a mugful and heated it in the microwave. McGraw was taking inventory of every convenience in the kitchen—like he was pricing it for a yard sale.

He took the coffee black. "Why don't we start with your side of the story first, David—what really happened to you on the way home?"

"I'm not going to tell you anything," David said.

"In that case, hear this," McGraw said. "A farmer whose address is rural box seventeen on the County Road heard a woman scream out in front of his place after midnight last night. It woke him from a sound sleep. He looked out, thought he saw a car stalled on the road, and decided to call the Sheriff's Patrol. The call was clocked at twelve-twenty. But on account of the accident on the interstate, the patrol didn't pick up on it till daylight. I went out there myself with Addy Muller, drove him in fact. He was dead on his feet after

140

a double shift. But the farmer was pissed at how long it took the sheriff's men to show up. I'm telling it to you straight, David. . . ."

David didn't say anything. McGraw took a noisy sip of his coffee. "Addy remembered you kids on the beach and figured you might've been heading home about then. He remembered you lived in Oak Forest. He asked me if I'd like to look you up while he made the rounds of the hospitals. You were the one he remembered by name and school. He thought you were too young to be running with that crowd.

"You didn't want to talk to me, David, you didn't show much respect for the truth either. In other words, you were scared. I can see why.

"It turns out the woman was on her way home from work, tired, late, and she had to relieve herself. No traffic that she could see. She pulled halfway off the road, turned off the lights, and went in front of the car. Now wouldn't you like to take it from there?"

David was silent.

"David, there was a witness. You were driving at high speed, came out of nowhere just as she came around from in front of the car. You could have made sausage meat of her, and you didn't even stop."

"I didn't hit her. I know that."

"How do you know?"

"I just do."

"So what do you think happened to her?"

David shook his head.

"But you didn't care as long as you could get away."

"I did care, but I knew I hadn't hit her."

"You *knew?*" McGraw waited, breathing noisily, a snort.

"What happened to her, mister?" David could feel that terrible tightness in his throat.

"I'm not a doctor," McGraw said.

"Is she all right?"

"I wouldn't say that. Oh, no. But *she* is alive."

David caught the emphasis on "she." "You said there was a witness. Were they in the car with her?"

McGraw gave him the sad smirk of a smile. "No, David, *you* are the witness."

He wondered how that could be and then realized he had in effect confessed to McGraw. He'd been trapped. He had trapped himself. And he was all he cared about. Not the woman. She wasn't a real person to him. She was a scream, like a face he'd brought up on the computer screen.

"I want to see her," he said. What he wanted was to *feel* her, to flesh-and-blood feel her.

"You could have seen her at the scene. Now it's up to her whether or when she will see you."

"What am I supposed to do, mister?"

"Exactly what I advised you to do yesterday: go over to the Sheriff's Office this morning and give Deputy Muller your statement."

"And if I don't?"

"They'll come and get you, David. I can promise you that. The woman will swear out the warrant for your arrest."

And the arrest would be reported in the *County Sentinel*'s "Crime Watch." But the woman was alive: why couldn't he say thank God and mean it? He hated himself for what came into his mind and for saying it, but he did: "What if I asked you to represent me?"

"It's too late for that," McGraw said, sounding regretful.

"You're representing her, aren't you?"

"Such a smart young man, David, would you believe me if I told you I don't wish to represent either of you in a court of law? You will agree surely that you owe the unfortunate woman something simply on the strength of the information we have exchanged here this morning?"

"Isn't this some kind of blackmail, mister?"

"What a dirty word. No, David. I am offering you an honorable solution to something that could be very nasty. It could mess up your life, your career, people knowing you'd run away like that. What I haven't told you till now—the woman was pregnant, David. She miscarried after the accident."

David felt the message like a blow to the stomach. He had trouble getting his breath.

"I think we can call it an accident," McGraw went on, "but in her mind it was murder."

"I'm sorry for her," David said finally, and it wasn't associated with McGraw's mention of murder. It was for something lost.

"Sorrow's too cheap, David. Think about it and after you've seen Deputy Muller, let's talk again. She's a poor, hardworking woman. A settlement would not impoverish your family."

David watched McGraw down the driveway, the coat as he struggled into it swished out like Batman's cape. He tucked it around him as he got behind the wheel of a car marked SHERIFF'S OFFICE.

The woman was human, David thought, a human being, and the sorrow he felt was for her, not for himself. It was going to be McGraw's word against his, no matter what happened, he reasoned. Not that he was thinking of the lie he could tell to get out of his admission, but he wanted time to think about what he was going to do. He didn't think McGraw would make any move until he had turned himself in, until he signed something saying he had left the scene where someone might have been hurt due to his reckless speed. He was trying to tell himself the truth, the way it was now. In a way, he had hit the woman and he wanted to go back and pick her up. He couldn't do that, but if he could find her, he could ask her to listen to him, and he could tell her he was sorry. Murder, he felt sure, was McGraw's word. It was meant to scare him. The funny thing was it didn't, but McGraw still did.

David knew he needed help. Maybe he did need a lawyer, but he just didn't think so. What he needed first was a private detective, something as remote from his experience as a TV melodrama. What he needed was his father. Not available. He'd recommend a lawyer anyway, and in spite of what his mother had said about David's being able to talk to him, he didn't think his father would be able to listen.

He drove to school and got to see Father Moran in his office. The priest shook hands with him, not the usual start of a student interview. He knew a troubled young person when he saw one. He told David to move his chair so the light wouldn't shine in his face.

"I got to thinking after yesterday's brouhaha," the priest said, "one of those what-if questions. What if, after hiding out overnight, Iscariot had showed up at the foot of the cross and said, 'Lord, forgive me.' "

David grinned. There was nothing to say and yet there was a lot.

"What can I do for you, Crowley?"

"I did a bad thing, Father." David told his story, even to having thrown the condom into the wind.

The priest lifted an eyebrow. "Standard equipment," he growled. It was the only comment he made until David was finished. Then, after a few seconds of thought: "And when you find her?"

"I don't know," David said. "I just want her to know I'm sorry for what happened to her."

"Even a decent lawyer would advise you against self-incrimination."

"I don't care!" David all but shouted.

"By the grace of God, I'm not a lawyer," the priest said. He took the phone book from the bottom drawer of his desk. "Let's start with the nearest hospital to where this misfortune occurred."

Within the half-hour he had the name and address for Alice Moss. When she hemorrhaged with the miscarriage, she had taken herself back to St. Vincent's Hospital. It was where she worked on the custodial staff.

"If you didn't hear me scream," the woman said after she'd thought about it, "how were you going to hear if something else happened to me?"

"I don't think I wanted to hear anything," David said.

Mrs. Moss scraped a bit of congealed egg from the table with her thumbnail. They sat in the hospital's employees' cafeteria, where midafternoon traffic was light. She did not in any way resemble the face behind the scream. Her salt-and-pepper hair hung in a clump at the back of her head. Her eyes were tired. She seemed confused, slow, but her question was on the mark. She twisted uncomfortably on the metal chair. "I don't like you coming to me like this," she said. "I'd just as soon never know you."

"I'm sorry," David said.

"You said that already and I believe you're telling the truth. But I think you're sorry over something I'm not real sure I feel the same way about. That lawyer got me all confused, telling me how I feel when I don't feel that way at all." She concentrated on ST. MARY'S COLLEGE, the lettering

145

on the breast of his sweater. "David—Mr. Crowley . . ."

"David's fine," he said.

"I'm not saying what I want to say, and maybe I should keep it to myself." She drew a deep breath and looked at him directly. "I didn't want to have a baby at all, but I'm a church person and I felt I had to go through with it. Mind, I could have been killed myself last night, I know that . . ."

"I do too," David said.

"And maybe that would have been murder, but I still couldn't call the other thing murder. I was thinking when I came back to work this noon: wasn't I lucky on both counts?"

Before the next Christian Ethics class David told Father Moran about his meeting in the hospital cafeteria.

"Did she forgive you?"

"I think so."

"You're lucky, my lad," the priest said. They reached the classroom door. "I have a word of advice for you, Crowley. One word. . . ." He waited.

"Yes, Father?"

"Abstinence."

Till Death Do Us Part

Kitty found him finally. He was out on the terrace, no place to be on such a night. He stood, his hands on the parapet, his face to the wind and the strange billowing fog. At times the whole galaxy of lights that shone across the park from Fifth Avenue vanished from sight. Mark leaned over the parapet and looked down, unaware—or not wanting to acknowledge—that his wife had come out from the party to look for him. The apartment was full of guests, most of them agency clients and among those some of the most successful writers in the country, and Mark was out on the terrace.

"I've been looking all over for you. People are asking where you are."

"Who?" he said over his shoulder.

"Oh, God. You're in one of those moods. I'm sorry if I interrupted you with Jonathan, but I could see him getting restless. He has no patience. I didn't want him to leave the party."

He mumbled something she didn't hear.

"If you must know, I didn't want him hurting your feelings."

"Or me hurting his. Or isn't that possible?" He half-turned toward her. "I was going to ask him if now that he has all that money, we can call him the Root of all evil. You interrupted just in time."

"Are you drunk?" He had played upon the author's name, Jonathan Root, and referred to the recent book contract Kitty had negotiated for him, seven figures.

"Not as drunk as I'd like to be."

"You're going to catch cold out here, and we don't need it this time of year. Please, darling."

November, with all the cheerful holidays coming up, he thought. He turned and faced her, his elbows on the parapet. She looked glamorous—and was!—a white beaded dress, one shoulder bare, the little sway of self-assurance, and those very blue eyes that, except for the sparkle, were to be seen only in his mind's eye at the moment. "It's you that's going to catch cold," he said. "Go in and enjoy your party."

"It's not my party. It's our party."

"No, Kitty. That mixed bag in there is all yours. I don't like to see people eating their hearts out."

"That's pure imagination, and you're wrong. Success rubs off. Believe me. Look at me! Am I not the perfect example? If you've got it, you'll get it. I'm going in now and I want you to come with me."

"In a few minutes."

"Damn you," she said and whirled around to almost collide with André Wilczynski, a young writer, mostly of poetry, who was both client and sometime employee. When he served as waiter on such occasions as this, Mark called him their poet in residence.

Wilczynski tried to hold the door for Kitty and at the same time balance the martini on his tray. He, too, had been looking everywhere for Mark. Kitty snatched the glass from the tray. "Let him come inside for it if he wants it."

Kitty swept indoors. Mark turned back to watch the fog. When the doors closed between him and the party, he could hear the singing wheels of the traffic below and the rev of a heavy motor when the bus pulled away from the stop at Seventy-fourth Street. Looking down, he could see the doorman—like a tin soldier blowing a thin whistle with a little toy taxi creeping into view.

"Shall I bring you another drink, Mr. Coleman?"

Mark did not answer, annoyed that the young man was still there.

"Are you all right, sir?"

"Bring me the drink, André. Straight up. No rocks this time."

Kitty, indoors and checking people's glasses, looked around for Tom Wilding, the agency's lawyer and Mark's longtime friend, thinking to send him out to persuade Mark in. He wasn't in sight either. There were sixty or seventy people in clusters about the room, and yet it wasn't crowded. She could see everyone. The apartment—on Central Park West—was the top floor through of a building that had gone up in the 1920s. The Colemans had kept its decor to the fashion of the day. Mark called it late Scott Fitzgerald.

Aware that her feet hurt but that she was going to have to carry things entirely on her own, she put on a jaunty air and moved among the guests. She encouraged the successful authors to hold forth and gave a squeeze to the arm of a listener who hadn't made it yet as much as to say, All this can be yours too. Among those whose careers were modest and who chose the company of their own kind, she would linger long enough to bring the conversation to where she could recount the meteoric success of an author—not present, but a name everyone recognized—who'd been living hand-to-mouth on minuscule advances until Kitty took her in hand.

Tom Wilding watched all this from alongside a pillar in the dining-room archway. He knew the script. He also saw the young man in a white coat that was too big for him take a single drink out onto the terrace. So that would be where Mark was and why Kitty was carrying herself around with a

149

brave tilt to her chin. What an actress she was: a royal presence moving among her subjects. Kitty avoided mirrors, he thought, and never looked behind. Therefore she didn't know—or didn't have to admit to caring—what people thought of her.

In a broad sense, Wilding had been watching Kitty for a long time, almost twenty-five years, from the time, he suspected afterward, she made her choice of whom to go after, him or Mark. To admit the truth, he had been briefly attracted to her, beguiled by her vivacity and those big blue eyes. He remembered taking a long look into them on the eve of her marriage to Mark. Whatever he saw then, it was not the Kitty of today. Nor was Mark the man he liked to remember. In those days Mark was considered one of the best young literary agents in New York. His authors loved him. Even publishers loved him, which might be the key to his eclipse—if that was what it was. Wilding had always considered himself lucky to have acquired the Mark Coleman Agency as a client for the legal firm in which he was then a junior partner. He hadn't known how lucky. Today he could live on the income from it. Which was the reason he could take the gaff from Kitty that he did. He often wondered how Mark took it. But he also wondered sometimes if Mark knew what he was taking.

About to light a cigarette, he thought of going out with it and joining Mark on the terrace. Kitty hated the smell of cigarettes. Wilding smiled at his motivation, but he proceeded on his way outdoors. Before he reached the terrace, he saw a scuffle going on there, a flash of the white coat and then the crash of glass as the young man flailed, trying to get his balance. Wilding ran to help him; so did others, the whole party rising to its feet.

Both of the French doors shattered, and shards of glass

seemed to explode. Wilczynski was instantly aglitter with them, and Mark still went after him and tried to pull him up by his lapels with the manifest intention of hitting him again. He threw off Wilding's attempt to get hold of him. "Get out of here, Tom. Keep out of this!"

It was Kitty who intervened and pulled Mark away. Wilding took Wilczynski through the gaping, gasping guests to the nearest bathroom. He had several cuts on one side of his face, the slivers of glass still in some of them. On the other side his jaw was swelling, a possible fracture. "Can you talk?"

"No." Which meant that he didn't intend to, Wilding thought, not to Coleman's attorney certainly.

"We'd better get you to an emergency hospital," he said, a proposal he hoped would assuage the man. "First aid is going to do it, but let's get it from a professional." He took him through the kitchen and out by the back hall. Their topcoats were jammed among others on a rack in the foyer. Wilding said he'd come back for them later. In the cab, which crept through the fog westward toward Roosevelt Hospital, he tried again to find out what had happened.

Wilczynski took away the towel he was holding to his face. "I'm not going to sue or anything like that, Mr. Wilding, so you don't have to worry."

Wilding held up a hand to forestall his saying anything more in that vein. "My concern at the moment is to get you to a doctor, and I don't think you should think about noble gestures in your present condition."

Wilczynski didn't speak for some time. He touched his jaw tentatively and winced. Then: "When I took a drink out to him, I thought at first—he looked as though he was going to jump off the terrace. Maybe it was all in my mind, but I started to talk him away from the ledge, saying how people like me needed him, things like that. When he realized what I was talking about, he came over and told me to put down the tray. He wanted to know what I'd suggest instead of the big jump. I wasn't going to say anything, but the way she'd humiliated him in front of me, I just let go: 'You don't have to take that shit, sir.' And whammo."

"I get the picture," Wilding said.

"I guess I'm lucky not to be on my way to the morgue."

Wilding said nothing.

"He shouldn't have asked me a question like that," Wilczynski said and buried his whole face in the towel.

The attorney waited until almost noon the next day expecting Coleman to call him. Then he called Coleman. "Any word from Wilczynski?"

"No."

"What got into you, Mark?"

"He maligned my wife."

"Just what did he say?" Wilding wanted his version.

"If I could remember, I wouldn't repeat it."

"You could be in serious trouble, Mark. Twenty-eight stitches. There could be disfigurement."

"I'd hate to see that happen. He's got a nice face—homely, but a good face. And he's a good writer if he could stay with it."

"I think you ought to apologize to him, Mark."

"Kitty says no, that I'd lose face. Which is pretty funny when you think about it."

"I'd better talk to Kitty," Wilding said reluctantly.

"She's waiting for you. Hang on. I'll switch you over."

Kitty came on the phone full force. "Most lawyers I know would advise a client to stay clear of the victim, whether it's an accident case or whatever. Our lawyer, it seems, commits us to instant liability."

"Would you have had him bleed to death out there on the terrace?"

"Was there nobody in that whole crowd who knew anything about first aid?"

"Twenty-eight stitches, Kitty. That's beyond first aid."

"You made sure of it, rushing him to the hospital. Just tell me where things stand now. Give it to me in words of one syllable."

Very slowly, making sure of his own composure, he explained the situation as he saw it. He knew very well that Kitty's point did have cold-blooded merit.

"So what's the big deal? He'll apologize."

"Kitty, just in case the worst happens and he does decide to sue, I want to apprise you of the way I think it might go. If it were ever to come to trial, whoever represented Mark would have to plead him mentally disturbed. Counsel would ask leniency, and the judge might grant it on condition that he undergo psychiatric care."

"He's been seeing a psychiatrist for years."

Wilding hadn't known it. So much for psychiatry, he thought. "Well, let's see what the apology will do. The warmer it is the better. And you might ask Mark to let me know if Wilczynski also apologizes."

"He will," Kitty said. "He's jealous of me and he adores Mark. We shouldn't represent him at all, much less make a household pet of him. He's like every poet I ever heard of, arrogant as Lucifer and nothing you can do for him is ever enough." Her voice became a purr of sarcasm. "But Mark has a conscience about impoverished talent. The more impoverished, the greater the talent."

"I'll be in touch," Wilding said.

Mark, at his own desk in his office, hung up the phone after listening in. It was something he was not in the habit of doing, but neither was he in the habit of throwing punches, not since the age of thirteen. He looked at his bruised and swollen knuckles and tried to think why such a blazing fury should have erupted in him. No answer came. He had known there was no love lost between Kitty and Wilczynski, but André had kept it under cover until last night, when, Mark had a sneaking suspicion, he had deliberately provoked the boy into letting go. But to say that Wilczynski adored him was one more of Kitty's exaggerations. And yet the very idea of it made him both sad and pleased—sad that he had struck him and pleased that someone among the agency's clients still held him in esteem. So why had he struck him? Still no answer. He could ask his psychiatrist—if he had one. Kitty's lies of convenience were a commonplace, but why it was convenient for her to tell Tom Wilding that he had been seeing a psychiatrist for years was one more thing he was at a loss to know.

He wrote André a note in longhand and mailed it himself when he went out to lunch. Kitty was furious. Not even a photocopy, with the machine sitting right outside his office door. "You should have spoken to me sooner," he said.

"I thought we agreed you were *not* to apologize," she said.

"Did we?" he said blandly. "Then I changed my mind."

"So did I. But I'd like to know what you wrote."

"I apologized."

Kitty turned on her heel.

Tom Wilding went out of town that afternoon. He had already told Kitty before the party that he would be away for a few days attending his son's wedding. It was a bittersweet occasion for Wilding because it brought him together again with his former wife, whom, despite her desertion and remarriage, he still loved. During the flight he pondered from time to time how that could be, given his anger, jealousy, pain, and humiliation, the embers of which still flared up now and then. He had not even realized when it was happening. He had been on the Coast a great deal and, the children in college, Irene had gone back to school and taken her master's degree. He'd been very proud of her. There was in his musings a barely conscious comparison of his situation with Mark Coleman's. He was comparing apples and oranges, he told himself. Irene had not emasculated him, although he felt it at the time, and he had put together another life without her. The Colemans were somehow bound together in their needs. They had simply switched places. Supposing Irene had stayed with him and got a law degree? He laughed at himself and rang the stewardess for another Scotch.

The next afternoon, while the wedding party was at the church rehearsing, he and Irene sat before a fire together. She had not changed save for the scattering of gray in her soft brown hair and a few new laugh lines. There came a moment when she looked at him with warm concern in a way that made him ache, remembering. "And how is your life, Tom?"

He was all but overwhelmed by the urge to tell her of his loneliness and what her leaving had taken from him. "I'm enjoying it," he said, and the temptation passed.

Whenever he thought about the Colemans between then and his return to Manhattan, he would wind up trying to pinpoint the place and time when their rise and fall intersected, where in plain fact Kitty had taken over and Mark had let go. She had come to New York wanting to be an actress and was in acting school when Mark met her. She started in the office working part-time in the Dramatic Rights department; Mark thought it would give her confidence as an actress to learn something of the business end of things. He was jubilant when she was able and wanted to take over the department. That wasn't long after they were married. Her next step upward was becoming a member of the firm, and after that the question arose whether the agency name shouldn't be changed to include hers. She was adamant that it remain the Mark Coleman Agency. By then she might have thought she was the Mark Coleman Agency. Equality seemed never to have entered her mind. The only good word she had for the women's movement was for those of her clients who wrote about it. Wilding tried to remember what Coleman was like in negotiations at given times along the way. More and more, he could see now, Mark had left the gritty bits to him, the legal expert. Kitty, to the contrary, would tell Wilding what she expected and, outrageous as it might seem, she almost always got it. She was an exhausting negotiator. Only once recently had he been with both Colemans in the same negotiations, and by then Mark had lost much of his personal prestige and his perspective. He insisted on explaining to Kitty points that she knew better than most of the people present. She listened him out, however, and smiled with cold defiance at anyone less patient than herself. She would defend him to the death from others, Wilding thought, and then turn on him and savage him herself.

One of the first things he did when he was back in the office was to find out if there had been an exchange of apologies. He would rather have talked to Mark, but it was Kitty who had promised he would apologize. "Mark wrote him," she said, "and purposely didn't show the letter to me. What do you think of that?"

"Understandable," Wilding murmured.

"He kept no copy of it—wrote it in longhand. Is that also understandable? And no word from André in the meantime, at least according to Mark. What's going on there, I'd like to know?"

"Let them sort it out between themselves, Kitty. Give it a little more time."

"Tom, the more I think about it the more bizarre the whole situation seems to me. It isn't like Mark to engage in fisticuffs. Between you and me, I can't see him doing more than telling André to keep his opinions to himself: I suppose what I'm saying is, I don't think I was the issue at all."

"I don't know what to say to that. Why don't you give his psychiatrist a ring and have a confidential talk with him? He might find your input useful."

"I suppose I could do that," she said. "I'm glad you're home. How was the wedding?"

"All brides are beautiful. It was very nice."

That afternoon Wilding got André Wilczynski's phone number and called him. A purely personal concern, he explained.

"No complications," the writer said of his wounds. "How is Mark?"

"I wish I could tell you. I've been out of town and out of touch with him."

"Why don't you try and help him, Mr. Wilding? That man's in trouble. Do you know what he wrote to me? I haven't answered it yet, I don't want her getting hold of it and twisting what I say into what she wants me to say. That's pretty complicated, isn't it?"

"What did Mark say?"

"He said he was hitting out at himself, and I just got in the way."

"That *is* complicated," Wilding said. "A very peculiar traffic jam."

Wilczynski laughed, and Wilding was glad that he

could—in more ways than one.

Coleman had surprised himself in writing as he had to André. It was almost as though he had let out something from his soul in automatic writing. But reading it over, he had known it was the truth and sent it off. When days passed and he had not heard from the young writer, he wondered if he had made a fool of himself. Or worse, if he had not compromised Kitty. When Tom Wilding called him and suggested lunch, he was sure something had gone very wrong. They had not had lunch alone together for years.

They met at the Century Club and had a drink at the bar before going into the dining room. Mark's hand trembled as he conveyed the glass to his lips, and he said again something he had already said far too many times about the first drink of the day: "It's nice to be drinking again." He turned to Wilding. "You've heard me say that before maybe?"

Wilding laughed and admitted that he might have.

"Does Kitty know we're having lunch?"

"Not unless you told her," the lawyer said. "There's nothing heavy on the platter, so relax."

Mark could feel the relaxation happening. He turned his glass around and around by the stem and said, after a moment, "I wonder if these things aren't doing me in. I forget things. I say things I don't mean. Sometimes I even say things I do mean. I flare up—as you may have noticed. I blame Kitty . . ."

"For what?"

Coleman shrugged. "For more than she ought to be blamed. God knows, she takes good care of me."

Wilding took a chance. "Is that good?"

"Have you been talking with Wilczynski?" It was said not seriously but with a twinkle reminiscent of the old Mark.

Then: "I thought he might have answered my letter by this time. I suppose you know, I did apologize."

"He'll answer. He intends to."

"But when? Kitty wants to see it in writing."

At the table, when Coleman had his second drink in hand, Wilding said, "Mark, I'm going to make a suggestion. Give this thing time. Take a few days off and get away from the office . . ." He paused, seeing alarm in Coleman's eyes.

"Why?"

"I was thinking how much good it did me to get away and see the family, people I hadn't seen in years."

"I see too many people. I'm sick of people and I'm sure a lot of them are sick of me."

"Then how about this: Go up to my place on the Cape. This time of year it's nothing but sea and sand and stars. It's as pure a place as you'll find on earth."

Mark was instantly thrust back in place and time to the graceful sand dunes along Lake Michigan where he'd grown up, Carl Sandburg country, a poet all but forgotten, as were most of the poets of his youth. He blinked at Wilding across the table and said, "I've just had a short trip—back home to Indiana."

"What about the Cape?"

"I can't get away, Tom. I've got too many things in the works."

Wilding clamped his mouth shut.

"Go ahead and say it," Coleman challenged.

"You can't get away from Kitty. That's what it's all about." Wilding pulled back. "I'm sorry. I shouldn't have said that. That's for your psychiatrist to say, if anybody's going to say it."

With a smile that was almost self-satisfied, Coleman said, "I haven't had a day of psychiatry in my whole damn life."

Wilding was speechless. He felt that even the breath had been knocked out of him. After all the years of Kitty watching, he still had no idea of where her facile tongue might dart. "Might it not be a good idea, then—a few months of therapy? With the right man, of course. Or woman."

Coleman missed the unintended irony. He had scored with himself for having again told the truth instead of fudging on it to cover Kitty's lie. Then it occurred to him, causing him some anxiety, that there could have been a reason for Kitty's saying he was in psychiatry: It put a wall up around him, as it were, to protect his privacy.

"Not that it's any of my business," Wilding added. "I presumed on a long friendship."

"Psychiatry invades everybody in the patient's life. I wonder if Kitty might not take it as an insult."

"For Christ's sake, Mark. I'm talking about you, not Kitty."

"The same thing, isn't it?"

They were back to square one. Mark had stopped any censure of Kitty before it started. Wilding gave up. There was no way to help a man who would not be helped.

After lunch, which both men found a strain, Mark put the lawyer into a cab and made his own way uptown through the swarming Christmas shoppers on Fifth Avenue. Salvation Army Santas were cleaning up, so were the vendors and the street musicians, who had to blow on their hands to keep their fingers nimble. Only the blind man, whose dog lay on a mat at his feet, was missing out. On the crowded sidewalk in front of Saks, people didn't see him in time. Mark stepped off the curb, dug all the change from his pocket, and went back to put it into the beggar's cup. It was a gesture that seemed to have perfect logic—if symbolic logic could be perfect. Something had happened with Tom Wilding at lunch that at the

160

time gave him the smear of pain and satisfaction he usually found euphoric. But the pain lingered when the euphoria wore off. He had seen a longtime friend cut loose from their attachment.

Kitty was exasperated at her inability to come to terms with the Mark-Wilczynski incident. She, who was herself one of the greatest stonewallers in a business where such talent was indispensable, was wearing down under the failure of the situation to resolve itself. She imagined all sorts of changes in Mark. For example, he was not as responsive to her in bed as she had come to expect. But that might be the booze. And if there had to be a choice between the two, she'd rather it was the booze than Wilczynski certainly.

She walked into Mark's office the day after he'd had lunch with Wilding, giving him only a moment's notice as she came down the hall. Two of the younger associates were putting up Christmas decorations, and she stopped for a word with them. Mark smiled up at her from a desk as neat as a jelly-bean. The smile was false, she thought, meant to deceive, to distract her from something. It's a Christmas present, she tried to tell herself, something he'd just managed to hide. She could tell that to someone else, not to herself. On the desk in front of him was a folder advertising a survival knife, the illustration a jagged, lethal-looking weapon.

"Christmas shopping?" It sounded as false as his smile had looked.

He threw the folder into the wastebasket. "I'd like to get away for a few days, Kitty. Tom has offered me his place on Cape Cod, and I might take him up on it."

"Now?" Her mind raced to what she could remember about Wilding's beach house. In summer it was private. This time of year it would be isolated.

"I was thinking of next week."

She watched the little pulse start at his temple. All so casual on the surface. Inside he was in turmoil, she could tell. He couldn't lie to save his life. "Would you like me to go with you?" She succeeded in sounding as though she was suddenly enchanted with the idea.

"It never occurred to me that you'd want to." His voice was as flat as the floor.

"I do want to, but darling, I can't get away, and neither can you. Janet Caruthers will be here from London next week, and I'm counting on you to cope with her. You said yourself it would be disastrous to submit her manuscript as it is now. When did Tom offer you the beach house?"

"We had lunch."

"You've heard from Wilczynski, haven't you?"

"I expect to. I thought I might ask him to go up to the Cape with me. He knows more about the outdoors than most people."

She could not believe her ears. What kind of a fool did he take her for? As naive as himself? "Mark, did he or did he not insult me? What's this business: 'He maligned my wife'? Give it to me straight out, what *did* he say?"

"Actually, it was me he insulted, only I didn't look at it that way at the time."

"*What did he say?* The exact words: spit them out."

"He said I didn't have to take all the shit."

"From me?"

Mark shrugged. Who else?

"The insolent pup. To dare to speak to you like that. Or is that among the privileges you've given him?"

"What does that mean?"

"Mark, do you see what you're doing to me? You're rewarding him for what he said."

"You're forgetting, I almost killed him that night."

"Too bad you didn't," Kitty said. "One more botched job to your credit."

Back in her own office Kitty phoned Wilding. "What in hell are you trying to do, break up my marriage?"

"That would take an act of God, Kitty."

"What about Wilczynski?"

"What about him?"

"Is there something going between him and Mark?"

"Sexual? It would never have entered my mind."

"Then think about it: You offer him a house on Cape Cod, and he decides to take Wilczynski with him."

"I didn't even know he was taking me up on the offer, Kitty."

"He's not. Believe me."

"Kitty, don't jump to conclusions. That's a really off-the-wall notion about Mark and Wilczynski. It's father and son if it's anything besides agent and writer."

"If you're holding back on me, Tom, I'll cut your heart out."

Mark had heard from Wilczynski. When Kitty left him, he retrieved the survival-knife flyer from the wastebasket by way of occupying himself until it was safe to resume what he'd been doing when she came into his office. He watched her out of sight and then kept his eye on the phone lights until he saw that she was at her desk and busy. Then he took the manuscript from the middle drawer where he had swept it out of sight on her arrival. He had heard from Wilczynski and found the communication a great deal more disturbing than not hearing from him had been. Some thirty pages and a brief outline had arrived from him that morning with a covering letter that read:

Dear Mark:

I think you know that I have wanted to divide my time and talents in such a way that I can earn my living by writing. I like the idea of poetry and the murder mystery, but until our recent bloody encounter I could find no satisfactory act of violence on which I could take off.

Please let me know what you think of these few pages and whether you would consider working with me on the plot. I've heard Kitty boast about working with her writers, so that I don't hesitate to ask. You may consider this beginning an impertinence, but if it is, it's a devoted one.

André

P.S. I am sending a letter to both you and Kitty under separate cover. It should clear the air.

The locale of Wilczynski's proposed novel, although said to be in a building on Riverside Drive with a view of the Hudson River, was plainly the Colemans' apartment on Central Park West, which André knew startlingly well. The principal characters, crudely drawn in this beginning, were comparable to the Colemans only in that they were a married couple approaching middle age. The woman was fat, long-suffering, and bland, and kept a meticulous house, nobody recognizable to Mark. The man had a Mephistophelian quality. "A cross between Mephistopheles and Svengali," André had written. Which, Mark thought, did not leave much room for character development. Mark had suddenly realized what Wilczynski was trying to do when Kitty walked in on him: He had switched the roles of the Colemans. It did not bother Mark much to see himself portrayed as a tub of lard, and under other circumstances, Kitty might enjoy the role into which she was cast. But the whole gambit disturbed him, especially with murder as its objective. However, if André could write suspense, he should be encouraged and helped to find a different vehicle. Without Kitty's knowing of this beginning. It was with this in mind that Mark had briefly entertained the notion of going to the Cape after all and taking Wilczynski with him, and had tested it out on Kitty. Patently he was not going with Janet Caruthers about to arrive. He put the Wilczynski proposal—to describe it a more advanced way than it deserved—into an agency folder and stashed it in a desk drawer. He decided to do nothing about it until the other letter André had mentioned came.

Wilding came out of a meeting to take Coleman's call. Mark hadn't said it was urgent. The sense of urgency was his own. Kitty's conjecture about Mark and Wilczynski had distressed him. She was an unpredictable woman, and he didn't like to think what she was capable of doing if something of hers was threatened.

But Mark was quite cheerful. "Kitty said you wanted to know: We now have a letter of apology from André Wilczynski."

"Read it to me if it isn't too long."

"Very brief in fact." The pertinent line read, " 'I hope you will allow me to consider my punishment sufficient to the offense.' "

"Fancy words," Wilding murmured. They did not sound at all like Wilczynski. "But they'll do as long as he signed the letter. What does Kitty say?"

"I'll tell you exactly what she said, 'Okay. Now let's get rid of him.' "

"I'd do it, if I were you. I'd get on the phone right now and tell him in the most diplomatic way possible that while you accept his apology in the same spirit as he accepted yours, you think it would be better for him to find other representation."

"No. I can't do that, Tom. And to tell you the truth, I don't see why I should."

Wilding, aware of the suspended meeting awaiting his return in the next room, could not think of a judicious way to persuade Mark in the time at hand. "It's up to you. But for God's sake, don't lose that letter."

"It's safe. It's in Kitty's hands."

Mark postponed further thought about the Wilczynski proposal until the Janet Caruthers visit. He spent most of the weekend going over her manuscript. He thought it barely literate, but he would not say that even to Kitty, abiding by his habit of loyalty to his authors. He had merely told her that it needed work, something to which she agreed on rereading it. The problem was to persuade Caruthers that she owed it to herself to do some rewriting. Her publisher might well accept the book as it was, she was that popular. Mark felt good about himself and the work he did on the script. He was able to concentrate for long stretches, which, he would be the first to admit, said something for the Caruthers manuscript as well. Kitty was right: Literacy wasn't everything.

Caruthers arrived in New York Monday noon. Mark did not see her until Wednesday evening, when, at Kitty's suggestion, he took them both to dinner at Le Perigord. As soon as he had ordered cocktails, Kitty announced, "Janet and I have made a pact: Tonight is trivia time. Not a word about *Storm over Bertram Heights*. Don't you love that title, Mark?"

He said that he did and looked around to see if they were getting his drink. It was usually mixed and chilling by the time he'd given up his topcoat and seated his guests. It occurred to him that if Kitty and Janet had agreed not to discuss the manuscript, they had probably already discussed it. "What are we going to talk about? Am I allowed to ask since I wasn't in on the arrangement?"

Kitty flashed him a warning glance. He was not to be contentious. A quick smile followed. "What?" she repeated, an invitation to suggest a subject.

"Other writers—who's in, who's out," Caruthers said. She was a big, amiable woman, getting bigger with every success. She did not like to write especially but, as she put it, she had a knack for it and she loved the little luxuries writing could buy. It turned out she had spent the afternoon at Kenneth Beauty Salon.

Which information, along with the arrival of their cocktails, cheered Mark up considerably. There was something reassuring about having a client who spent the afternoon with Kenneth.

Mark scraped his last oyster from the shell. The women were slower, having champagne with theirs, vulgar or not, as Kitty said. He found himself free-floating, as it were, adrift in their easy conversation. Kitty was the heroine of all her stories, and he marveled at the attention authors paid her, even Janet. A kind of fairy tale.

Kitty, for her part, was quite aware that he was drifting in and out of their presence, speaking only when spoken to. He was still an attractive man, she thought: They were noticed wherever they went together. And she liked it that way. His silence troubled her, as though he'd gone off secretly on his own. She wasn't sure she wanted to know where. During the clearing of the oyster shells, she pondered how to reach him. She waited until the *Roti de Veau a la Maison* was served and their guest involved in her gastronomic adventure. Then she said to him, almost casually, "Mark, would you like me to try to place a collection of André's poems with Linden House?"

He came to instant attention. "I thought you wanted him . . ." He avoided saying the word *out* in Caruthers's presence.

"Obviously you don't," Kitty said. "And I thought you'd be pleased at the idea."

"Why Linden House?" He was shaken by the suggestion. And it was not a publisher he'd have gone to with poetry. Nor would he go to any house with as thin a body of verse as Wilczynski had so far produced. Kitty didn't even know what there was of it, much less its merit. She was putting him on, Mark decided, wanting to see how he'd react. But why? In her phone conversation with Wilding, the one on which he had eavesdropped, she told the lawyer Wilczynski was jealous of her. Now, he realized, she was jealous of Wilczynski. It boded both ill and well if she was serious about placing the poems. Above all, it would take him off the hook in discussing with André the mystery-novel proposal in his desk drawer: To have his poems published by a reputable house would seem extraordinary to him, and the very possibility of it would melt his hostility toward Kitty.

"A hunch," she said about Linden House. "You know me and my hunches. I always play them." She laid a finger on the busy wrist of Janet Caruthers. "I had a hunch Janet would like the veal."

"I've never had an experience like it," Janet said happily.

Mark kept thinking of Linden House and who there would possibly be interested in Wilczynski. It would have to be someone in the upper echelon. Kitty always went to the decision-makers. He did not want to press her. She might turn on him in front of Janet.

Then Kitty said, "Mark, stop racking your brain. I only had the idea five minutes ago, but you'd better believe I can get him a contract if I put my mind to it."

"Now who are we talking about?" Janet asked, dabbing her lips with her napkin.

"A young poet Mark is fathering," Kitty said.

Caruthers turned to him. "Is he good? He must be or you wouldn't be interested in him."

"I think he is." Then he remembered: On the terrace the night of the party Kitty and he had exchanged words about Jonathan Root, and that was the Linden House connection. Kitty had switched Root there on a million-dollar contract. She was quite capable of going back to them and squeezing out a thousand dollars more for a book they might or might not eventually publish.

But why would she do it? To lure the poet away from him? Or had she done it *for* him? He looked at her across the table. Her eyes were wide, blinking in anticipation. She expected him to say he was pleased. So he said it and added that young poets needed all the encouragement they could get.

It was a crisp, clear night, and they decided to walk the few blocks to the St. Regis, where Caruthers was staying. They paused to look at the long sweep of lights up Park Avenue and the joyous punctuation of a Christmas tree every block for as far as they could see. The tree in the hotel lobby was full of old-fashioned ornaments, and the music sounded as though it came from a calliope. Janet invited them to have a nightcap at the bar, which had a new jazz pianist, and she knew Mark loved jazz. The Colemans declined—a working day ahead, Kitty said. Janet kissed them both, thanked them, and wished them a Merry Christmas.

"I don't envy you Christmas in Los Angeles," Kitty said.

"Is it true," Janet wanted to know, "red, white, and blue Christmas trees?"

"And pink," Kitty said.

169

"When do you get back?" Mark asked. Somewhere along the line he had missed the information that she was going to the Coast.

"Late spring. One of you will come over to London before then. It would be super if you could come together."

"You're flying home directly from L.A., is that it?" Mark said.

Janet nodded.

"And . . . *Bertram Heights?*" He mimed a spiral with his hands suggestive of something ongoing, unfinished.

Kitty took over. "Darling, Janet had lunch with her editor and all of them yesterday. They want the book *now.* I said you'd agree—if that's how they feel, they'd better have it. You do agree, don't you?"

"The point is moot by now, isn't it? Shall we go home?"

"There simply wasn't time," she said in the cab when he had not spoken by the time they passed Columbus Circle and headed up Central Park West.

He still said nothing.

"If you must know, Janet made the decision. She's very fond of you, but she doesn't like her agent playing editor."

He turned his head to look at her. "You have such a gracious way of saying things."

"I tell it the way it is," Kitty said. "The trouble with Janet is her head is getting as big as the rest of her. She writes such awful stuff it's hard to believe how popular it is." She laid her hand on his where it lay cold and gloveless on his knee. "It would have been a waste of your time, darling."

"When I could be playing agent," Mark said.

Kitty left the apartment early in the morning, going directly to a meeting outside the office. Mark, his nerves jumpy from too little sleep and too much to drink, walked to work through the park. There was the feeling of snow in the air, and he could smell horse manure from the bridle path; the ground was hard beneath his feet. He thought of the time when, as a boy, he had tried to dig a grave for a bird the cat had killed and couldn't because the earth was frozen solid. He'd put it in a shoebox and kept it in his room. One day he smelled feathers burning. When he looked in the box, the dead bird was gone. Neither he nor his mother ever spoke of it. Where had such silence gone?

In the office he tore up his notes on the Caruthers novel and sent the copy of the manuscript to file. Left in the drawer were the folder with André's projected thriller and the advertisement for the survival knife. The knife would require six to eight weeks for delivery. André's project could stay in abeyance. He got the tearsheets of Wilczynski's published poems—as well as a few rejects—from the file and put them on Kitty's desk.

At noontime he did his Christmas shopping and then visited Herman's Sporting Goods and bought two knives, one for hunting, a long narrow blade, and the other an all-purpose survival knife. It was its description that kept getting to him. He got through lunchtime without a drink by the simple means of going without lunch as well. He called Tom Wilding midafternoon and said he'd changed his mind again. He wanted to take him up on the loan of the Cape Cod house. He'd be ready to go up in the morning.

"It's not possible," Wilding said and explained that his caretaker would have to turn on the water and get the heat up. Saturday at the earliest. "Mark, are you going alone?"

He hesitated. "Is that part of the deal, that I go alone?"

"Of course not. I was only thinking that it may get pretty lonely up there for someone as used to the city as you are."

"That's what I want," Mark said, and arranged to pick up the key the next morning.

"It's impossible," Kitty said. "There are several things during the week that we really must go to."

He cut into her recital of the holiday festivities. "You'll get along. Tom will be glad to take you—any number of people—flattered."

"It's not the same. We've always been a couple."

"Or at least one," Mark said.

"What's that supposed to mean?"

"I don't know what it means to you. I only know what it means to me. If anyone should ask where I am, just say I'm drying out."

"That'll be the day. I suppose André is going with you?"

"What gave you that idea?"

"You said you were going to ask him."

"That was a passing thought at the time."

"It's none of my business," Kitty said. "I merely wondered." She took her glass to the bar. For the life of her she could not figure out what was going on with him. "There's time for another drink before dinner. Do you want to fix it while I light the oven?"

"André's your client now. He'll be devoted to you," Mark said, getting up.

"What's this business of your client, my client? They're all *our* clients."

"If you say so, dear. But I give you my word on it, André is not going to Cape Cod with me."

"I don't want your word on it!" She started for the kitchen but paused in the dining-room archway. "And I don't want him as a client. I'm doing it for you, if you must know."

Mark didn't say anything. There was a time he had thought as much himself: He wiped his hands on a cocktail napkin. They were cold and sweaty. He mixed Kitty's

Manhattan and then added a few drops of water to what was left of his first martini. The thought of drinking it gave him no great pleasure. One day at a time.

In the kitchen, the swinging door closed, Kitty phoned Tom Wilding at home and, not reaching him there, phoned him at his club. Wilding listened out her tirade against him for having suggested that Mark go in the first place—this time of year, his tendency to catch colds, his state of mind. After which she demanded that he call Mark and say the place had burned down or blown away, anything to forestall his going. She was frantic, and he thought for the first time in years there was some hope in the situation. Old Mark was standing his ground.

Finally he said, "Kitty, why don't you let him go? That's the only way to stop him."

"You and your goddamn riddles! You're two of a kind." And she slammed down the phone.

Friday promised to be the longest day in Mark's memory. He went into the office thinking that Kitty might stay home, as she often did on Fridays, to read manuscripts without interruption. She was in the office fifteen minutes after his arrival. She kept coming in to see him on a variety of pretexts, some with concern about what he was taking with him—and did he want her to pack for him? He did not. There was concern also for what he was leaving behind, unfinished agency work. It was with almost demonic intuition that she said, "What about your desk drawers? You're always sticking things away and forgetting them."

"Clean," Mark said. "I'll be leaving them as clean as a whistle." And at that point he decided that he had to take the Wilczynski proposal with him, or send it back, or take it home and bury it in his study.

On one of her sorties she announced that she had bundled off the collected poems of André Wilczynski to Linden House.

"So soon?"

"It's almost Christmas," she said, further implying the kindness of her gesture. She could not have read them; he was inclined to wonder if anyone would. He told himself that cynicism would get him nowhere.

"It will be interesting to see if you can pull it off."

"Oh, ye of little faith," she said.

When Kitty went to lunch—to ease his own mind and despite his practice of not telling an author of a mere submission—he called Wilczynski. He told him that Kitty had submitted his poems to one of the biggest houses in Manhattan.

"No kidding. You mean she likes them?"

"I like them," Mark said with asperity.

"It's great. It's just great," André said.

"It's by no means a hundred percent sure, but Kitty has a way with publishers."

"Mark . . . don't show Kitty that suspense thing I sent you. She's a smart lady."

"And I'm not smart?"

"I didn't meant that, sir." André reverted to formal address. As author to agent, he went on a first-name basis; as an employee, he called him Mr. Coleman. "I hope you'd understand what I was trying to do."

"If I understand it correctly, I'm not sure I want to encourage you with that particular vehicle. Mind you, if you can write suspense, André, I'll certainly work with you. But why don't I send this manuscript back to you? Have another look at it yourself: I'm going out of town for a few days' rest. I'll call you when I get back."

"Mark . . . the apology was all right?"

"Of course. Otherwise . . ."

"Mark, please give it another read. The people can be changed. It's the house and atmosphere and the puzzle at the end I want to hang on to. I'm very keen on it."

He wound up wishing he had not called André at all. He put the manuscript in an otherwise empty dispatch case to take home with him. In the late afternoon he picked up the rental car. He felt too edgy to drive through the midtown traffic, so he went uptown by way of First Avenue to Ninety-sixth Street, where he crossed through the park and drove south again. He made several passes at a parking place near the apartment building and finally got the doorman to guide him into it. Upstairs he put the Wilczynski manuscript on a shelf in his study with a number of others in photocopy. Kitty called his study the land of forgotten books. But that was not so. There was some material there he even knew by heart.

He packed before dressing for the evening, laying the sheathed knives at the bottom of the suitcase. Only one of them had meaning for him, the survival knife. He wasn't even sure why he had bought the other. Tom's place was bound to have every kind of knife he might need—except the survival knife. The new film he and Kitty saw in special showing was not good, but the stars were there, and congratulations flowed, as abundant and effervescent as the champagne. Everybody assured everybody else of Oscar nominations. It would have taken him several martinis to warm to the occasion, and he was drinking ginger ale disguised as bourbon and soda. Kitty asked him twice if he was really going in the morning. Even her proposals to help him get away, he realized, were meant to deter him, and the ultimate act of deterrence was the dispatch of André's poems. He was beginning to sweat with the strain of the evening, when Kitty looked at him and said, "I'd better take you home."

While he was undressing, he noticed the carton half-tucked in at the side of his suitcase: a bottle of Wild Turkey bourbon. He thanked Kitty and then, while she was in the bathroom, buried the bottle in the drawer among his socks. His sleep was fitful and dream-ridden. He dreamed of someone he called mother, only it was not his mother. But it wasn't Kitty either. Sometime before dawn Kitty left her bed and crawled in at his back. He stiffened everywhere except where, presumably, she wanted it to happen. A fierce fantasy raced through his mind: rape and he the rapist. All that happened was the sweat again, and Kitty left his bed as silently as she had come to it. He thought he heard her crying but pretended not to. If Kitty was crying, it was a last resort.

He showered and shaved and then decided not to take the shaver with him. Kitty had finally fallen asleep. He took his luggage into the vestibule before zipping it. He made instant coffee and toasted a slice of rye bread that scratched his throat when he swallowed it. He looked out at an ominous red and purple sunrise and wondered whether to waken Kitty or to let her sleep. It would be easier to get out the door by himself: He reminded himself not to forget to turn the key in the top lock: This was something that figured importantly in Wilczynski's script, he remembered. He hadn't understood it. He wasn't sure the writer understood it either. Very muddy. For a moment he thought of taking the proposal with him. He even thought of losing it. Which had to be his low point on the ladder of cowardice. He brought in *The New York Times* from the hall and turned to the obituary page. There was nobody he knew among that Saturday's deceased. He felt a little disappointed. He folded the paper neatly. If there was anything that got Kitty's day off to a bad start, it was a newspaper that looked to have been read before she got to it. He used the maid's bathroom; it wasn't used very much, their household help coming in three days a week, the cleaning crew once a month. The water, when he flushed it, looked pink, rusty. He thought at first it was blood.

When he returned to the kitchen, he took up the chalk, intending to write a note on the blackboard. But what to say? See you this time next week? See you soon? Love. He put down the chalk, having written nothing. He set out a tray with a cup and saucer, plate and napkin. And the bud vase. A large bowl of chrysanthemums stood on the dining-room table. There were always flowers there, and he would often pluck one out and put it in the bud vase on the tray. Did he do it for Kitty or for himself? He put the dishes away, pocketed the napkin, and took the tray back to the butler's pantry. He simply could not get going until he pushed himself. He took a handful of cigarettes from the box on the dining-room sideboard. It was years since he had smoked, but he remembered the comfort a cigarette used to be, a companion on a long drive alone. He could not remember his last cigarette or his last drive alone. He got his parka from the hall closet, his earmuffs, gloves, scarf, and keys. The only sound when he left the apartment was the heat starting up. In the lobby the night doorman was asleep sitting upright in a high-backed chair. A robot could have taken his place and done a better job. Mark let himself out without disturbing the man.

Kitty wakened a few minutes after eight with the feeling that she had been drugged, which was so: Valium at 5:00 A. M. He was gone, she realized, the bedding pulled down but left unmade, the heavy drapes closed, the room cold but too dry, always too dry. Another Saturday morning and he'd have brought her a tray by now—croissant if he'd been out—otherwise toast and fruit and dark fragrant coffee, Zabar's best,

177

and almost always a rose in the bud vase. He would draw the drapes to let in the sky, as he put it, and start up the music in the radiators. Very poetic. Which put her in mind of Wilczynski. "Shit and damnation," she said aloud. She got up and went from one room to another, just to make sure he was gone, her mules clacking on the hardwood floor, then muted on the heavy rugs, then loud again and with a faint echo as of distant hammering. She was tempted to give up her Saturday morning at the health club. But why? To do what else? She rinsed his cup and used it, the jar of instant coffee on the counter where he'd left it. Not even a note on the blackboard. She phoned Tom Wilding.

"I hope I didn't interrupt anything sexual," she said when he came to the phone short of breath.

"I have better concentration than that, Kitty. What's on your mind?" He had no intention of telling her that he was bicycling in place, and he never understood why he was the recipient of her sexual innuendos. Hardly innuendos, but they certainly weren't passes either. To him she was about as sexually attractive as a camel in heat, and she could think up something as revolting to say of him, he was sure.

"Could I have your Cape Cod phone number? He's on his way, you'll be glad to know."

"I'm sorry, Kitty. The phone up there's turned off for the season."

"If you're just saying that, I can find out some other way, you know."

"I do know. I also know that with winter storms—"

"Okay, I believe you," she interrupted. "More important—I have two seats for the Actors' Benefit of *Candy* tomorrow night. Will you take me?" *Candy* was the hottest ticket in town.

"I'd love to, Kitty—"

"Good. Pick me up at seven."

"—but I have a date," Wilding finished his sentence.

"You can break it. It's important for me to be there." She let a second of silence hang and then said, "So I'll see you tomorrow night." When she put down the phone, her hand was trembling. She had thought he was going to turn her down. Now, she decided, she would give him his Christmas present early—after the theater. Actually, she had bought it for Mark—an old English print of a court scene during the Restoration. She was sure Wilding would appreciate its worth, and it might just raise her stock with him a point or two. She would rather court than tomahawk him, but she knew she would never win him, and she didn't like herself for trying. From the day she had first trapped his eyes with hers, he had seen every black spot on her soul. He might even have seen some she did not know were there herself.

The masseuse inquired after Mark. She had met him once when she came to the apartment and thought him very attractive. Kitty wove a tale about his having gone to the north woods for a week of duck hunting. If he got his bag early, he intended to go farther north on a moose trek. There was great hilarity between the women on where to hang the moose head if he brought one home. Then Kitty admitted she was pulling her leg about the moose hunt. But she did promise her a wild duck for Christmas, thinking of the butcher shop on Madison Avenue that specialized in game.

She cabbed home greatly relaxed by the sauna and the probing hands of the masseuse. She admitted to herself that she might not know Mark as well as she had thought. He might very well come home in better shape than he had left. And, in truth, she looked forward to an evening or two with Tom Wilding. The one thing she wished she could do in Mark's absence was get rid of Wilczynski. He had become a ridiculous intrusion in their lives, a snot-nosed kid. She wondered if it was safe—legally safe—to undertake dropping him herself. She proposed to speak to Wilding about it, to have him compose the letter.

When she opened the apartment door, she smelled cigarette smoke, and that frightened her. Then she saw the suitcase, its contents spilling over the floor, shirts, shorts, socks. With the parka dropped on top of them. She found him in his study slumped in the swivel desk chair facing her, his face gray, his eyes glassy. The bottle of Wild Turkey sat on the desk unopened.

"What happened? Were you in an accident?"

"No."

"What then?"

"I couldn't go. I just couldn't go."

Her rage was explosive. She flung her pocketbook at him, the only thing at hand. "You weak, impotent fool!"

The pocketbook contents scattered on the floor. When Mark stooped to gather them, Kitty saw the knives on the desk, both unsheathed. Her fury subsided. "Mark?" She pointed to the knives.

He straightened up and swiveled to where he could pick up the knife with the jagged edge. "This one is called a survival knife. I thought it meant something. Not a thing." He threw it down and took up the other with the slick, long blade. He used it to break the seal on the whiskey bottle. "You know, it's funny—I thought you'd be glad to see me."

Kitty brought two glasses from the teacart, the portable bar. She took the bottle from his hand and poured them each a drink. Touching her glass to his, she said, "Welcome home," and threw down the whiskey. She picked up the two knives and started from the room with them.

"Leave them," Mark said.

"Where?"

He shrugged.

She put them in a manuscript box on a shelf near the door.

Mark gave her a sad little smile. "Whatever else is wrong with me, Kitty, I am not suicidal."

A few days later, on Christmas Eve, Wilczynski called the office to see if Mark was back. An office party was in progress, so that the person answering Mark's phone didn't bother to inquire whether or not he wanted to take the call. "It's for you, Mr. C.," she called out, and Mark soon found himself explaining how, at the last moment, he'd not been able to get away after all.

"I don't suppose there's any word yet on my poems?"

"It's too soon, and Kitty would have told me," Mark said. "Do you need money?"

"That's not why I called. I wanted to wish everybody a Merry Christmas."

"Thank you, André. But *do* you need money? You don't have to keep a stiff upper lip with me."

"Just read my pages again and see if we can go to work."

"I promise to do it over the holiday."

"Mark, are you sure Kitty was serious about getting my poems to a publisher?"

"Absolutely," Mark said, but even as he said it, he felt his heart drop down.

"I don't mean to be ungrateful, but I'd like to have put them together myself. The order makes a difference, don't you see? And not all of them should go in. Would you ask her? I've retyped and arranged them, and I'd be glad to bring them in on Monday."

"Call me first thing Monday morning." Mark had a terrible feeling, hanging up the phone, that Wilczynski was wiser in the ways of Kitty in this instance than he was. She had moved with impossible haste.

He kept waiting for the right moment to approach the subject. Kitty did it for him. They were home in pajamas and waiting for the delivery of barbecued spareribs, chips, and onion rings, when she said, "Did you tell André I was showing his things to Linden House?"

"I didn't mention Linden House."

"But you did tell him something?"

"I did, yes."

"Well, now you can have the pleasure of telling him I've changed my mind."

"You can't do that to him, Kitty. I can't do it. Didn't you tell me you'd already sent them to Linden House? You did tell me that."

"I told *you* that. I didn't tell him. I wanted to see if it was really good news to you. And it was. Oh, yes, it really was."

Mark was too upset to say anything.

"Don't you see, this snot-nosed kid, this two-penny poet of yours is fucking up our lives?"

"They were pretty well fucked up before he came along. Oh, Christ." He poured himself a double shot of gin and drank it straight.

"You do hate me, don't you?" Kitty said.

"Sometimes it isn't hard."

"You can't live with me and you can't live without me, right?"

He sat down, his face in his hands, and tried to think how to deal with Wilczynski. All his poems retyped, all his hopes recharged.

Kitty twisted her fingers into his hair and pulled his head up. "Get rid of him, Mark. Or I will."

He pulled away from her. "No. I've promised to work with him on a project and I don't intend to let him down on that. But I agree; he's better off out of the Mark Coleman Agency."

Wilding read the draft letter, dated January 5, to Kitty over the phone. It was much along the lines of what he had proposed Mark say to Wilczynski in a phone call. "Mark should sign it, you know."

"And if he won't?"

Wilding thought back to the day he'd advised that Mark apologize and Kitty's saying, No problem. "I thought you said he agreed to the severance. I'll talk to him."

"What I want is to sever the relationship entirely. This thing they're working on it's an excuse. That's all. I see them out there in Central Park, walking up and down like a pair of lions in their natural habitat. Oblivious to traffic, to weather . . ."

"Kitty, get rid of the binoculars."

"Don't be such a smart-ass. There are a lot of hungry lawyers in this town."

"God knows, I'd wish them bon appetit," Wilding said.

Kitty ignored the remark. "He's obsessed with this ridiculous person. And it's not as though he has talent. He calls himself a poet, therefore he's a poet. I couldn't submit stuff like that if I'd wanted to. And I did want to. Sort of."

"Did you read it?"

"My secretary read it."

Mark had said she hadn't, and she hadn't. There were moments Wilding could almost feel sorry for her, but they were rare moments. "I'll talk to Mark," he said.

"If you can't reach him just say your name's Wilczynski."

Mark and Wilczynski, huddled in their overcoats, sipped

their tea in the drafty zoo cafeteria. Little tornadoes of dust and leaves were dancing outside the glass enclosure. André was saying that he thought he could now take the story, which he'd call *Till Death Do Us Part*, from there without Mark's help. At least till he got to the locked-room situation. "You've taught me an awful lot, Mark."

"It may turn out that *awful* is the precise word for it." He leaned back and enjoyed the realization that working with André had been a great pleasure—the quick and probing mind, the eagerness to work, to rework.

"One thing you taught me," André said, "Henry James wasn't a mystery writer."

Mark laughed and said, "Drink your tea and we'll walk back to the apartment and run through the lock business on the scene."

"Couldn't we just work it out on paper? I don't want to meet Kitty."

"She's at the office," Mark said. "One member of the firm has to support A.T. and T." He got up. "And if she were home—so what?"

André mimed cutting his throat.

They were skirting Tavern on the Green when André said, "Mark, did a publisher really reject my poems? You just said they were rejected. Was that Kitty?"

"Yes. She was wise enough to see that you aren't ready yet and to withdraw them. There's not a publisher in the city with whom your record isn't entirely clean."

"Good old loyal Mark," Wilczynski said and gave him a hug.

Kitty had not intended to be home that afternoon, but something at lunch had disagreed with her. Or else she was coming down with a bug. In any case, she wanted an instant cure, having to carry most of the office burden alone these days. Once home, she certainly did not intend to go out on the terrace with binoculars. She had acquired them after Wilding's wisecrack, a figure of speech on his part. But she did go out. It was cold and raw and windy, and she really did not care at the moment if she got pneumonia, for no sooner did she have the glasses in focus than she picked up the two men coming toward her. It was at the moment Wilczynski threw his arm across Mark's shoulder.

When they got out of the elevator, Mark illustrated his usual procedure on arriving home. He rang the buzzer—two longs, two shorts. "If Kitty were home, she'd answer and probably let me in. And vice versa if it were I who was home . . ."

"What do you mean, probably? That's not good enough."

"Don't be so fierce," Mark said. "We'll work it out. Let's say I was in the habit of forgetting my keys sometimes. And say I phoned to tell her I was on my way home and had forgotten them. She'd be sore as hell at me, but when I buzzed my two longs and two shorts, she'd yank the door off the hinges to confront me. How's that?"

"Mark, that's exactly how I had it in my first version, the one I sent you. Transpose the sexes and it goes like this: She throws the door open to you, only it's not you. It's a burglar, a killer. He'd stolen your briefcase in the park with all the notes you'd made on this thriller you were going to write . . ."

"Who then does the real job for me," Mark said. "And look . . ." He illustrated the two-lock system: "This is what's called a warded lock. You have to turn the key in it to open it and, once in the apartment, you have to turn the key to lock it behind you. The tumbler lock is automatic. Now the fact is I've been known to go out in a hurry and simply let the door lock behind me on the tumbler lock. I sometimes forget the one I have to turn around and diddle with. Kitty's right. I am careless."

"Then it's simple," André cried. "Let's say you've called her to say you forgot your keys. She tells you that she's not surprised because you left the top lock off again. You say, mea culpa, hang up and start for home in your own good time. When you get there, you do the buzzer routine, two longs, two shorts. No answer. You hang in there, thinking she may have fallen asleep. You try again. Then, really panicky, you run down the stairs, get the super, and he comes up with his big ring of skeleton keys. Right? You keep urging him to find one that's going to fit the top lock. He finds it, but—the shocker—he didn't need it. The lock was off all the time. But Kitty never, never leaves it off. Which means she must have opened the door to someone, thinking it was you, someone who afterward let himself out, with the automatic lock falling into place when he closed the door. The same as when you forgot your keys. You and the super get the door open, and there she is, lying in a pool of blood."

"Jesus," Mark said.

"Cold blood," Wilczynski said. "It's all in the script. All we have to do now is work out a time schedule."

"And write the book."

"You do know you're the major suspect till they pick up the guy who stole your briefcase?"

"I can live with it," Mark said.

In his study Mark got out the manuscript and outline—or, as he had called it then, the proposal. While Wilczynski read it aloud with flourishes and flying spittle, Mark poured each of them a drink. They toasted *Till Death Do Us Part* and set to work on timing the mayhem schedule.

Kitty came almost to the door of Mark's study in her

stocking feet. She glimpsed both men, André at the desk. Mark leaning over him, his hand on Wilczynski's shoulder. She saw him give André an affectionate little poke on the chin, with André leaning back and saying, "Hey, that's where all this started!" Great laughter. She had almost forgotten what Mark's laughter sounded like. She heard her name mentioned, and that was enough. She fled to the bedroom, undressed, and buried herself in bed. Time passed. Darkness and silence. When she got up and crept through the apartment, she saw that they had gone out again. She checked the door. Typical: Mark had forgotten to turn the lock. She got her own keys and locked it. Then she went into his study, lit the desk lamp, and opened the middle drawer. A creature of habit, Mark had cleared his desk and put the work in progress in the middle drawer. She read every word of it and saw herself instantly as the cross between Mephistopheles and Svengali. She left his study as she had found it, leaving the vestibule light on, and went back to bed.

Mark was surprised to find her home. She had come in a few minutes ago, she said, and felt so miserable she decided to go right to bed. She reprimanded him for leaving the door half-locked.

"Isn't that just like me?" he said. "And do you know where I was? I went looking for a locksmith. And by the way, it's time we updated our security system." He leaned over and kissed her cheek and said he was sorry she wasn't feeling well. He even smelled like Judas, she thought, although she knew that what she smelled was the spice he chewed to cover the whiskey on his breath.

Kitty was scheduled for a breakfast meeting in Boston that Thursday. She had first intended to take the early shuttle flight but decided on Wednesday to go up that night and stay over at a hotel. She was not working well and she needed all her wits to try to salvage a contract a publisher claimed the author had violated. Going early meant she could not attend a dinner party Wednesday night for the benefit of the Writers' Colony, an annual gala event at which she and Mark were often photographed as being among its celebrities. There was a time when missing it would have grieved her. Now she felt only a twinge of anger at not being grieved. Mark said he would put in an appearance at the dinner, and she immediately wondered if that meant he would go off somewhere with Wilczynski as soon as he could get away.

She stopped home to pick up her overnight case after speaking at the Columbia University seminar on "The Business of Writing." The word *business* Mark had wanted out. He also seemed to have opted out of the office that afternoon as well. He was at his desk, the study door open, the wire basket at the side of his chair half full of typescript, where, for the sake of speed, he dropped each page as he read it.

"Is that you, Kitty?" he called out as she was locking the door behind her.

"Who else?"

She stopped for a moment at his desk, and they exchanged a few words about the seminar, Mark rhythmically, automatically, and blindly continuing to leaf the pages of manuscript into the basket.

"That must be a great book," Kitty said.

Realizing what he was doing, he laughed and fished the unread pages out of the basket. "Monumental," he said.

In the bedroom she noted that he had already put out his dinner jacket, dress shirt, and black tie, and for an instant she was tempted to reverse her plans again. A seesaw: Her life had become a seesaw, she on one end, Wilczynski on the other,

Mark the hump in the middle. She put a fresh blouse in the case for the morning and closed it. If she hurried, she could get in a couple of hours at the office before leaving for La Guardia. She was touching up her makeup when the phone rang. Mark took the call on the third ring. He was still talking when she set down her purse and overnight bag outside his door.

All she heard at first was a couple of grunts, cheerful, humorous sounds. She had no doubt at all as to who was on the phone. Then Mark said, "As long as you've got a tux, wear it. But no sneakers, hear me, boy?" He saw Kitty then and finished off "Seven-thirty, just inside the Fifth Avenue door. Okay?"

"I'm not going," Kitty said when he'd hung up the phone.

"You're not going to Boston, is that it?" He glanced at her and quickly away.

"That's it. So you'd better call him back and tell him you're taking your wife to the dinner, not your mistress."

Mark sat for a second or two, grappling with the concept. Then: "Jesus Christ!" He got up and went to the teacart, where he poured himself a drink. He did not want to look at her, not the way she was now, her face distorted and blotched with anger. "I could get down on my knees and swear," he said. "But it wouldn't do any good. You couldn't believe, could you, that I had in mind how important it might be for him to meet the Colony trustees? He ought to try for a fellowship."

Kitty hardly knew what she was doing. A raging instinct sent her to the manuscript box in which she had put away the knives on the morning he had not been able to go to the Cape. The hunting knife in hand, she meant to force her will upon him, nothing else. "Are you going to call him?"

Mark took his drink back to the desk, still averting his eyes from her. "I'm going to think about it," he said and drank the whiskey down.

She even challenged him: "Look at me, Mark."

He shook his head.

When she came up behind him, he might have thought she would yank his head up by the hair again. Instead she plunged the knife into his back and left it there. He slumped forward onto the desk, and then when the swivel chair rolled out from under him, he fell to the floor. By then Kitty was at the door. She caught up her purse and overnight case only to set them down again twice, once to open the vestibule door and once to lock it behind her. There was no way she could stand and wait for the elevator. She ran down the stairs, floor after bare-walled floor, her knees buckling and then steadying sufficiently to carry her on. She stood at what she thought was the door entering onto the lobby and tried to pretend that it was all a nightmare, and that beyond the door she would wake up. She opened the door and found herself not in the lobby but in the basement, a few feet away from the laundry room, where she could hear the chatter of women and the raucous laughter of a neighbor whose voice she recognized. She went out the service entrance and then walked as fast as she could toward Columbus Avenue, a very long block from Central Park. The cold wind of February tore at the coat of her three-piece suit and then reached in to catch at her throat.

A crime of passion, a crime of passion: The words kept racing through her mind. I didn't want to kill him, she tried to tell herself, but she did and she knew it. The very thought of him and Wilczynski going to the dinner set her aflame again. She began to feel justified and instantly then to wonder if it were possible to escape discovery. The doorman might not even have seen her come home. She had bussed down from Columbia and entered the building while he was putting someone in a cab. And no one had seen her leave just now. Only Mark knew that she'd come home. She looked at her watch. Well under an hour ago. If only she had not double-locked the door, she might get away free. She realized it was their very script that she was going over in her mind! The top lock was to be left off as though a burglar/murderer had been admitted by mistake and after the crime had simply walked out of the apartment and closed the door behind him. She had even followed the instructions about going down the stairs and, inadvertently, out through the basement. She turned back, determined to go in as she had come out of the building. If she were seen, she would brazen it out somehow. Her writers called her the great improviser. She expected Mark to be discovered by their cleaning woman in the morning, who would arrive at ten o'clock and let herself in, noting as she did so that the top lock was off again. A born tattler, she never failed to let Kitty know when Mr. Coleman had forgotten to double-lock the door.

Wilczynski, of course, might try to sound an alarm when Mark failed to show up at the Colony dinner. By then she would be in Boston, with only Mark and her secretary knowing where. The police would do nothing before morning.

She was unable to return to the building through the basement, because the entrance was locked from the inside. She stowed her overnight bag in one of the empty ash cans, where she could pick it up later and thus not be encumbered with it now. She went around the building to the corner of Central Park West, from where she watched with agonizing patience the doorman popping in and out. Then God—or the devil—was with her, for a school bus came and dispersed several children into his charge. Kitty went into the building by the side entrance as the youngsters were going around and around in the revolving center door. Mothers and nannies tried to snatch and sort them out. She reached the elevator ahead of all of them, pressed the number for the second floor below her own, and went slowly upward entirely alone. Entering her own vestibule from the stairwell instead of the elevator, she found it a foreign place. The naked aluminum coat rack—unused since the November party—made it seem a desolation. It would never be home again. The sorrow of it welled up in her, the tears making it difficult for her to see to put the key in the lock. She intended to go, having turned that one key, but the overwhelming feeling hit her again. She felt that once she opened the door, she would step out of the nightmare, home safe. But when she did open it, she knew the nightmare was forever: Mark, lying on the floor, had gathered himself to himself and died in the fetal position.

Kitty tried several times to dial Tom Wilding's number but got it wrong each time. Finally, she simply dialed 911.

Miles to Go

Laura set her weekend bag, her purse, and the gifts of chocolate creams—one for her aunt Mattie and one for her father-in-law—by the hall door. She tucked a scarf into the pocket of her reversible jacket where it hung on a hall tree and went to find her husband. You could smell the paint throughout the apartment, and God knows, the whole apartment needed painting. It was in anticipation of a financial gift from her aunt Mattie that they decided to go ahead with the paint job now. Tim wanted to see how much he could do himself while she was away.

The paint bucket gave a perilous shudder as he came down the ladder. Much better for her nerves, Laura thought, that she was getting out of the house. Tim stooped low and Laura stood on tiptoe to kiss him. He was a tall man and she had to stretch to make five feet two. They were both crowding middle age, married for almost twenty years. No children. Alas! both of them always added. Tim worked variously in the entertainment field, a magician who built his own illusions, a folk singer who improvised modern metaphors on old legends. He made most of his living in summer camps. He was what those with scorn for the race—or so much pride in it they could not abide mere affinity—called a professional Irishman. Laura was a lay teacher of English and music at a convent school just up the Hudson River from New York. The Mallorys owned the apartment on the Upper West Side, partnered to be sure with Chemical Bank. Large and high-ceilinged, it was full of books, the tools of Tim's trades,

193

and quite a number of things having nothing to do with modern employment, such as a spinning wheel, a loom, and a butter churn streaming now with ivy. Laura would be driving home from Vermont with the grandfather clock that had been in her family for more than a hundred years. It was a trip she cherished. She loved to drive. Tim was barely tolerant of her Honda, a 1993 Accord LX coupe, feeling it was built for Japanese midgets. He liked to say that if they had put the front seat in backward, and he lowered the back of the rear seat so that he could extend his legs into the trunk, it would just about fit him. Otherwise that convenience was great for a Christmas tree or, in the present circumstances, for the grandfather clock.

"You have the map and a flashlight," Tim started his usual rundown. "Take the cellular phone. I'll only get it all paint if you leave it here."

"I don't need it, Tim. Aunt Mattie would say it's an affectation."

"So is a grandfather clock."

"Tim . . ."

"Okay, okay. Just drive carefully. It's a car, not a palomino pony you're driving. If it starts to rain skip the hospital. You can call them when you get to your aunt's. And call me when you get there. Promise?"

"On my palomino," she said.

When they reached the door he said, "Give Dad my love. I'll write him soon. And mind you don't commit us with the hospital people, not yet."

"Wasn't it decent of them to let me come today?" Laura said.

"They can't wait to see you," Tim mocked. "I'll expect you back Sunday night."

Laura had taken that afternoon and Friday off. Friday was

St. Patrick's Day and most of the school was going to the annual parade on Fifth Avenue. She tried not to show how eager she was to get away. "I wish you were coming with me."

"To watch the speedometer," Tim said.

He waited at the apartment door until the elevator arrived, an ancient carriage of brass and wood paneling. A prickle of anxiety caught at Laura as she touched the lobby button. It passed with the door's closing and she put it out of her mind.

Once in the car she was in her element, secure. She made a U-turn out of the parking space and headed for the West Side Highway, accelerating to beat the first traffic light. The car seemed to anticipate her, leaping ahead. "Go for it, baby," she said, and patted the puffed-up center of the steering wheel, fat thing. It carried its air bag like a pregnancy.

The river was pewter gray and choppy with only occasional tugboat and barge traffic. Most of the pleasure boats were still in dry-dock. She could remember snow on St. Patrick's Day. This part of the drive was familiar, her school-day route. Yet she rarely drove it without seeking something new to weave into the pattern of her day's work. It was not easy to match imaginations with the young.

When she passed her usual turnoff, her mind went solely to the first stop on her journey. Tim didn't have to tell her not to commit them to the care and guardianship of his father. Guardianship? He hadn't used the word but it had occurred in their communication with the hospital. She and Tim had talked for years about the possibility of taking his father into their home when the authorities considered it feasible. When Aunt Mattie decided to give them their inheritance before her demise, they could no longer weigh their finances into the decision. The moment of truth was near. She was not afraid of the old man; nor was Tim. If Tim feared anything, it had to do with being his father's son. Joseph Mallory had killed a

195

man and had been confined for the past fifteen years in a psychiatric hospital.

Word would get out that Joseph Mallory was living with them. It had been a well-known case at the time. She had sat in the courtroom among a passionate lot of Mallory partisans. They brought him oranges and cigarettes, and the bailiffs allowed the gifts to be passed along. The courtroom had to be cleared when Mallory was found not guilty by reason of insanity. They had wanted him exonerated.

By the time she turned off the Taconic Parkway the sky had grown lumpy with clouds too swift for the rain, too heavy for the sun to part. The hills were a tawny stubble, patched with the brown of early plowing, the green of winter wheat. Greening willow trees hung over the reservoirs. It was almost spring.

The hospital gates were closed. On regular visiting days they were open, a larger staff perhaps. The gatekeeper came out of his shelter and checked her identification. She signed his register and tried to fix in her mind his direction to the Administration Building, where she was expected. Groundsmen were raking leaves. Traffic was sparse, mostly delivery trucks. Signs pointed to Laundry, Rehabilitation, Workshop, Drug Center, a Children's Unit. It always surprised her that there was a children's facility in a place like this. Their building was like the rest, dusty yellow brick. Not a swing or a jungle gym in sight. She drove into the Administration lot and parked the Honda among cars more expensive than itself, most with MD license plates.

It was not until she was waiting alone in the reception office that she remembered the chocolates she had brought her father-in-law. She had left them in the car. The question of whether to go back for them was settled when the attendant said Dr. Burns's secretary would be right along. Dr.

Burns was superintendent of the hospital. When the attendant turned his back she could see the outline of a gun and holster beneath his uniform jacket. She looked up quickly to the one picture on the wall, a huge golden eagle with the American flag clutched in its talons. This was a terrible place, she thought, to call a hospital.

Dr. Burns's secretary was male, all male to judge by his size and the shoulders that shaped him like a triangle. He did try to accommodate his step to hers as they clattered down the corridor. She could hear the broken rhythm of her own footfalls. "Do you know Mr. Mallory?" she inquired.

"Uncle Joe? Oh, sure. Everybody knows Uncle Joe. He's a card."

There didn't seem to be anything else to say. "I brought him some candy and then left it in the car."

"He's not much for sweets as I remember."

"What could I bring him that he'd like?"

"A songbook maybe. He's taken up music lately."

Dr. Burns, too, spoke of Joe Mallory's turn to music. "We got him a violin and he's taught himself to play it. He's very good—I'm something of an amateur musician myself." The hospital superintendent took her from his office to a small adjoining sitting room—plastic chairs, ceiling light, one window, and a small round table with a white chrysanthemum in its center. Burns was a rumpled-looking man with tired eyes and a mustache that needed trimming. Laura thought a violin would become him. "I've sent for Mr. Mallory. You'll be comfortable in here and you and I can talk afterwards. I wouldn't mention to him what you wrote me. Unless you already have?"

"No."

"Time enough."

Laura was looking out the window when two men came in

view, one wearing a white hospital uniform, the other a heavy sweater that looked to weigh him down, Joe Mallory. He had to skip a step now and then to keep up with the orderly. She waved when they were near, and the old man saw her. He pulled himself up and saluted, military fashion.

He was even more jaunty when he came into the room and held out his arms to her. She said it to herself every time: If she had not been at the trial, she wouldn't believe this man could commit murder. They pulled up two chairs to the table. Mallory took the white chrysanthemum to the window. The sill was too narrow. He set it on the floor. "Flowers should come in colors," he said, and pulled his chair closer to hers. "I've never got over the Easter lily they gave me to carry on Holy Thursday. The smell of it made me sick and I threw up right in the middle of the procession. You came alone again, did you?"

"Tim sends you all his love."

"There must be more of it than I'm getting," the old man said, "or it wouldn't be worth sending." He blinked his very blue but rather cold eyes at her. "Is he ashamed of me? It's far too late for that. I get letters to this day from people saying they're proud to have known me. And me with no recollection of them at all." He glanced at the office door and leaned toward her. "I think they're intercepting any letters I get now. I'll tell you why in a minute. And listening in on everything. If we was to turn up this table, do you think we'd find one of them listening gadgets? Or in the blossom I took from the table? Oh, I'm serious. If you was to look on the other side of that door, you'd see Leroy sitting there, his chair tilted to the wall, and his ear bent to the crack. He's the one brought me over. His name isn't Leroy, but I call him that. You have to feel superior to somebody in this place that isn't in a worse state than yourself. Do you think Tim's afraid of me—my bucking boy who pretends he's an Irishman when it suits him? I don't like a man who denies his blood."

"But he doesn't deny it, Joe. He was born in this country, remember."

"Will I ever forget it, the death of his darling mother."

"That's not fair," Laura said softly. Tim was hard enough on himself for all the sadness in his life.

"Then I'm the blame!"

"Must there be blame?"

Mallory sat back in his chair. He puckered his lips thoughtfully. "You're a soft woman, Laura. He's lucky. I wish I'd seen you first myself."

Laura was straining to be natural. "Is it true, everybody calls you Uncle Joe?"

The old man chortled, more at her clumsiness, she thought, than at the benevolence of institution and residents. "Somebody must have started it and the rest picked it up and passed it around. You know I've been studying the law. Did they tell you that?"

"And the violin," she said.

"Oh, they'd tell you that all right, but not about me informing myself of the law in as rare a case as mine—as the law was fifteen years ago and is today. I learned the ins and outs of it pretty damn well. Then I wrote the governor a masterful petition for retrial. I pointed out that the insanity plea on which I was acquitted would not stand up today. Whereas if I'd been convicted of murder in the second degree I'd have been eligible for parole two years ago. I was a pawn of the politicians. I had a court-appointed lawyer with a brogue as thick as you'd hear in County Mayo. He thought himself a genius getting me put in here instead of the brig. And me a hero. Oh, yes! The blow I struck was for Ireland when I cleaved his skull in two. He was on the docks and supposed to be handing off the occasional crate of rifles marked for Arabia to them who'd see them transported to Ireland . . . ."

Laura had heard him tell the story before. He told it often, filling in more and more details that were utterly blank to him at the time. Certified by three psychiatrists. The transport worker he killed had betrayed the very men to whom he was handing off the munitions: he was that dread character in Irish lore, an informer.

"So what does the governor say?" Laura eased the question in.

"I've not heard a word, and my informant in the bureaucracy here tells me the bastards never sent him the petition at all. That's enough. I'll not spoil your visit. Time is no longer of the essence to me as it must be to you. It was grand of you to come. Is it the same little car you have?"

"It's my love," she said.

"I can understand that. Where is it again you're going?"

Laura explained.

The old man pushed away from the table. "I'm going to ask Leroy to run back for my fiddle. I'd play you a tune before you go." He pulled open the office door without knocking. The orderly was sitting, his chair tilted against the doorframe, even as Mallory had foretold of him. "So you see, I'm not paranoid," the old man said, returning to the table. "We're supposed to stay close as Siamese, him and me, but there are privileges to be had if you know when to behave and when to act up. Do you follow the news, Laura?"

"Not as closely as I'd like to."

"Come on, girl. If you wanted to follow it closely, you would."

Laura nodded.

"Do you believe there's going to be peace in Ireland now?"

"I hope so."

"Would you rather peace or justice?"

"Why can't there be both?"

"Well, they've sent a fellow over here now who'd say you're right, and he's getting a hero's welcome—a new fashion in heroes." He looked about as though for a place to spit.

A few minutes later the orderly returned and handed in the violin case with the admonition "You don't have much time, Uncle Joe."

"As though I have anything else," the old man said, and took the violin from the case as tenderly as he might a baby from its cradle. He tuned the strings to a pitch pipe he put back in the case.

The orderly returned to his tilted chair and closed the office door three quarters this time.

Mallory tightened the bow and started to play. The tun were out of a beginner's manual—"Humoresque," "The O Refrain." Laura was moved that he had wanted to play for I and pondered again what it would be like if he came to I with Tim and her.

Mallory tuned one of the strings while Laura said I good he was. He winked at her then, tapped a martial with his foot, and sawed the strings in a wild lament tha more a wail than a melody. Bagpipes could not screeched worse.

Both the orderly and Dr. Burns burst in from the The old man, a gleam in his eyes, kept playing until t derly confronted him, hands half clutched. Mallory till the last minute and then handed over fiddle and b

"They'll be waiting for you, Uncle Joe," the order He put the instrument in its case.

Laura's father-in-law came to her, his hands outst He pulled her to her feet and kissed her on the mouth

to the gate with you, darling, if they weren't waiting for me in Babel." At the hall door he imperiously motioned Leroy out ahead of him. He turned and threw Laura a kiss.

She remembered the chocolates again. Again too late.

Dr. Burns joined Laura in the sitting room as soon as Mallory and the orderly had gone. He closed the hall door. "Would you rather talk here or in my office, Mrs. Mallory? People come and go in there. Better here perhaps. How did you find the old gentleman? He looks well, doesn't he?"

"Is he not, Doctor?"

"Not my meaning. He takes good care of himself. With our help, of course." While he spoke he retrieved the chrysanthemum from where Mallory had set it on the floor and put it on the table again. Laura wondered at the possibility of a listening device. Surely not. Once again she sat at the little table. The doctor straddled a chair. "You didn't mention to your father-in-law your inquiry about his possible release?"

"No."

"I wonder what his reaction would have been. He likes it here, you know."

"That's hard to believe," Laura said.

"Well, for one thing, he's top banana." Dr. Burns laughed a little. Not easy for him. "He taught me the expression—top banana. He talks about his son being in show business. Says he taught him all he knows. And he is clever. I'm not sure what to say to you, Mrs. Mallory. There are times—" He broke off when his secretary came in bringing two mugs of coffee. "Here we are. Sugar and something like milk can be provided . . ."

"Just black," Laura said.

"Not exactly down home. You've met Tony? Yes, of course, when you arrived. Thank you, Tony. I'll be available in a few minutes, tell them if they're waiting for me."

The secretary retreated into the office and Laura said that she had to go soon, that most of her trip lay ahead of her.

"Miles to go before you sleep," the doctor quoted.

She nodded and sipped the coffee, bitter as alum.

"We do review your father-in-law's case periodically, you understand. I've said he likes it here. I'm not sure that's true. He's a great manipulator."

"He's an Irishman," Laura said.

The doctor smiled. It was spontaneous and she liked him better. "What about these Irish fraternal organizations he talks about? He gets letters from them now and then, harmless things, like 'Cheer up, the world's not getting better waiting for you. . . .' We used to censor mention of Irish politics, but with things looking better, and he is allowed newspapers . . . but what I want to ask you: Would any of these organizations help you support him?"

"I don't know. I don't even know the names of them except when they march on St. Patrick's Day."

"That's coming up tomorrow, isn't it? Let me get Mallory's file. Do you want more coffee?"

Laura shook her head and said, "Thank you." Her cup was more than half full.

"Don't throw it in the plant," the doctor said. "It's had its quota for the week."

Laura leaned back and relaxed for the first time since arriving. They were human here after all. Which, strangely, made her want to reconsider the enormous undertaking of making a home for a man who had been institutionalized for fifteen years. She remembered the dog Tim and she had bought from a kennel. They got it cheap because it had been living in the kennel for two years. The first day in the house it bit Tim and wouldn't let him come near Laura.

Dr. Burns was gone for several minutes. She could hear

him on the telephone and sounds within the building seemed to be picking up, muted bells and intercom messages. She supposed that, as in all hospitals, they had their evening meal early. Daylight was fading and it looked as though it might be raining. She did not know why but she did not want to get up and go to look out the window, and she thought of the moment of fear in the elevator, at home, and then of a tale from her adolescence involving an elevator: "Room for One More." One thing about growing up, you didn't enjoy getting spooked anymore.

The doctor returned, apologized, and forgot to bring the file with him. He called out to his secretary. But just as Tony came into the room, an alarm sounded on the intercom system. Laura could feel the shock of it at the back of her neck. It was an eerie repetitive hee-haw, like the bray of a donkey. Both men stood still and counted. The signal was repeated. Dr. Burns excused himself to Laura and instructed the secretary to stay with her, but to monitor communications. He returned to his office, half closing the door this time so that Laura could only see him go toward his desk and soon come back from it. She wondered if he had stopped there for a gun. "Check seventeen, will you?" he said to Tony, and left by the hall door.

Laura knew from having written Joe Mallory that Block Seventeen was part of his address. She followed Tony to the door of the office. He watched her, waiting for his call to get through. The braying signal let up. She could hear her own heartbeat drumming in her ears. Tony spoke on the phone and then listened for what seemed a long time. Laura leaned on the frame of the door. The secretary signaled her to take one of the office chairs. She remained standing at the door. When he hung up the phone he said to Laura, "Mr. Mallory is in his room."

"Thank God," Laura said, "and thank you for telling me."

"It could be a false alarm. That's happened before. I'm sorry you had to get caught in it."

"I don't think I ought to wait for Dr. Burns. . . ."

The secretary was shaking his head. "The building's sealed. Nobody leaves just now. Why don't you sit down again? I'll bring you a magazine or two. Can't keep them in here. They disappear."

Laura was not going to remember a single word she read. What kept going through her mind was that they had checked out Joe Mallory. That had to mean something, some appraisal of his behavior. But what? And it was strange how they had broken in on his playing a dirge. If she didn't get away soon, she would backtrack on the whole idea of taking him into Tim's and her home. A few minutes later one long bray came over the alarm system. Tony came to the door and said he'd been right. It was a false alarm.

She waited another twenty minutes. Dr. Burns had not returned. Alarms must upset the inmates. Not inmates, patients. It was ridiculous but her nerves were getting ragged. She looked into the office where the secretary, his back to her, was working on a computer. She put on her coat and simply walked out the hall door and down the corridor by which she had entered. The guard checked her pass and opened the heavy door to let her out into a drizzle of rain.

The Honda was sitting alone, the cars with MD registrations she had parked between were gone. When she got in, she patted the steering wheel. "Oh, baby, am I glad to see you."

There was even less traffic on the grounds than when she had arrived, but lights had come on in all the buildings, and she told herself she ought not let her imagination run wild. It was a shabby thing she had done, leaving without a word. A

205

little more courage and she'd go back. No way, not tonight. At the gate she was required to sign out. A state trooper got into his cruiser and with a wave to the gateman, followed her off the grounds. As soon as they hit the highway, he turned on his flashers and passed her, picking up speed. "Follow that car!" she said aloud, and wished she could. Not on a winding, two-way road. She intended to go on to the Taconic Parkway, but to get away from traffic decided on Route 22 for part of the way. It was getting dark too soon. In the rearview mirror she saw that the sky was brighter behind her than ahead. She also saw a car turn in where she had turned. He gained speed until he was almost up to her. She slowed down to let him pass. He slowed down. She accelerated. So did he.

"We didn't need this," she said, again aloud. She did not like driving scared. She settled for fifty-five miles per hour; so did the driver behind her, and the uneasiness let up a little. She had read somewhere that fear and guilt went together. *Mea culpa, mea culpa.* It wasn't as though she'd let Joe Mallory himself down. Not yet anyway. She braked suddenly when a rabbit dashed into the road. It zigzagged in front of her, and kept to the road. Finally, she doused her lights. A pale, damp twilight. When she turned them up again, the rabbit was gone. But the driver behind her had kept even pace. There was a car behind him now too. She hoped it would follow him until she could get to the village ahead. Then, as they approached it, she decided to take a chance that he would turn off there. He didn't but the car behind him did, and she was soon beyond the village. She was in farm country, hollows in the road and fog she drifted into and out of. The rear of the car gave a thump. She didn't think she had hit an animal. It came again. She slowed down and checked the dashboard. Normal. Then she looked in the rearview mirror.

In the light of an oncoming car, she saw Joe Mallory palely, a face without a body. She swerved wildly, the right wheels jolting off the pavement.

"It's Joe Mallory, for the love of God," the old man called out. Stowed away in the trunk, he had pushed down the back seat and was pulling himself through the opening. "Keep us out of the ditch, girl!" and when she braked, "Don't stop!"

The Honda thumped itself back onto the pavement. Laura's mouth was so dry she couldn't speak. Her hands quivered on the steering wheel. Behind her the old man was struggling out of a white jacket such as Leroy wore. The car behind overtook them and slowed down alongside.

"Wave him on or I'll kill him," the old man shouted.

Laura waved. She did not look, afraid to take her eyes off the road. The driver gave his horn several jolly beeps and sped into the night.

Mallory pulled the coat off. "Free at last! Free at last!" he sang out. "I'll crawl up with you in a minute. Have you no radio in the car?"

"No."

"Mother of God."

Laura coaxed saliva into her mouth. "I park on the street overnight. The one in my last car was stolen."

"Savages." Then: "What did that sign say?" They had come up on a road sign and passed it.

"I didn't notice."

"Damn it to hell, I'm here without my glasses. Where are we?"

"On Route 22, going north."

"I don't want to go north. Turn around the first chance you get."

"Let's go back," Laura said. "You shouldn't be here, Joe.

207

They'll never let you out and Tim and I asked if they would soon."

"The hell you did, and him never writing to me. Don't lie to me, girl. They wouldn't even send my brief to the governor." A hand with fingers like talons grasped her shoulder. "I'm not going back so get it out of your head. I never heard of Route 22. Keep going ahead till I get my bearings. Isn't it a wonder I'm here at all?"

Laura didn't say anything.

A brief silence. Then she thought he was chuckling. "The key in the very place I taught him to hide it when he was a kid. They don't make bumpers like that anymore, but it was there."

Laura knew what he was talking about although she'd forgotten: After she had once locked herself out of the car, Tim had soldered a pocket on the underside of the bumper.

"Drive easy, I'm coming up front with you." He reached forward and put something on the passenger seat, a small, snub-nosed gun, terrible to see in the pale light of the dashboard. She wanted to grab it and throw it out the window but she was as afraid of the gun as she was of him. She opened the wrong window and closed it. He cursed the headrest as he twisted around and came over feet first. Sneakers, thin pants, and a sweater. His knees on the seat, he put the gun in his pocket and pushed the back of the rear seat into place, closing the trunk.

"Bastards won't even give you a belt to hold your pants up with." He wriggled around, a slight, wiry figure on the seat beside her. But deadly. Or was he?

"Is the gun loaded?"

"Ha! Would I carry a dummy?" He giggled and then laughed. He rocked back and forth in the seat, the laughter bubbling out of him. It quieted down to a cough. Finally:

"You want to know where I got it, don't you?"

"No. I want you to throw it away and let me take you back." Once she had spoken she knew she could speak, and it occurred to her then, she had a mighty weapon of her own, the car, the Honda, which Tim said would go through hoops for her. "Listen to me, Joe. Dr. Burns asked me if some of the Gaelic organizations—the ones who wrote to you—he wanted to know if they'd help support you if you came to live with Tim and me. Now do you believe me?"

"Tell it to me again. My ears are stopped up."

She repeated more or less what she had said.

"Bloody spy. He was looking for information. Did he say the word 'Gaelic'?"

"He did," she lied.

"And what did you tell him?"

"I never got to tell him anything. The alarm cut us off."

He was on the verge of laughing again. He choked it back. "And me lying in my bed innocent as a babe."

"Yes," she said.

"What do you know about it? Nothing. I was under the bed, and Leroy rolled up like a pig in the blankets."

Dead? she wondered. She wondered also at the strength and agility of the man beside her. The orderly must weigh nearly two hundred pounds.

"What are we going this way for? Read me the road signs we come to."

Laura missed the next ones purposely; chief among the directions was that to the Taconic Parkway. She said she was sorry, and began to contrive a desperate gambit. When the next sign came, it also pointed to the Taconic. She read it aloud, but took the road in the opposite direction.

"How long before we'll make the city?"

"Two hours."

"They'll be looking for me with dogs by then. Is there no way you can go by side roads?"

"I can try. Where do you want me to take you?"

"Aren't you taking me home? Isn't that what you said you came for? Won't Tim be waiting for us?"

"Okay, Joe. Let's go for it." She drew a deep breath and took firm hold of the steering wheel.

"I'm pulling your leg, girl. Isn't that the first place they'd look? You'll put me down near the heart of the city, and I'll get lost among my own. I'll have a night on the town." Once again he broke into high, hysterical laughter.

Laura, trying to watch both him and the road, came up too fast on a broken-down car, the driver outside it trying to steer and push it off the road. She swerved wildly and must have missed the man by a hairbreadth. She could hear him screaming after her. She could only hope he'd contact the police. Rolling with it, she straightened the Honda.

"You did that on purpose, didn't you?" the old man said. "You could've cracked my skull. You could dump me on the road and be off to Vermont or wherever the hell you're going."

"I'm taking you home," Laura said grimly.

"There's a tune to that. I wish I could've brought my fiddle. I don't wish that at all. It'll be alive and well when I'm writhing in hell. Ah, Laura, there's times I wish I could pray. . . ."

"We could pray together," she said.

"Not if you knew what I'd pray for."

"What?"

"That I'll find the motherless bastard who sold out Ireland for a penny's worth of peace."

"Oh, my God . . . Don't, Joe. Ireland's not worth it!"

The old man didn't hear her, intent now on his own reso-

210

lution. "If I live through the night and the parade is to-morrow, I'll send him home in a coffin."

There was no way he could make it, surely. And yet, he had found a man seventeen years ago, after a four-year search for him.

The rain had almost stopped and the sky to what she supposed was the south was a musty yellow and pink. She turned toward it.

"What's that ahead making all the color?" he wanted to know.

"New York."

"It lit up the sky when I was on the run there. Can you go no faster?"

She sped up and, glimpsing the speedometer top seventy, passed two cars, and shot between a third and an oncoming truck, her wheels squealing.

"You're a Barney Oldfield!" the old man shouted.

He twisted his scrawny neck to look after a passing sign. "Where are we now?"

"Near Yonkers," she said. It was a familiar name, though they were miles and miles away from there.

"Cows?" said Mallory. "Did I see a cow?"

"An ad," she made up. "Borden's milk."

"And no more traffic than this? What time is it?"

"Look at the clock." It wasn't seven yet.

"I can't read it. Do you have a pair of glasses I can try?"

"Try my reading glasses. My purse is on the floor at your feet."

He plundered her purse while she sped on, praying to attract police attention, but there was no traffic at all. She thought they'd soon be in reservoir country and she'd have to slow down.

"I've money in my pocket I saved all these years," he said.

"Will you go to the police as soon as you leave me?"

"I don't know."

"If you don't know, who does?" He was trying her glasses. "Can't see through the damn things at all." He put them back in her purse. "I've lived my life, Laura. Half dream, half horror. You wouldn't begrudge me a last hurrah?"

"What about Leroy?"

"Leroy. What about him?"

"Did he help you escape?" What she had wanted to ask was if he had killed him.

"Not by choice. He'll sleep till they wake him. I put every pill in my box down his throat." Mallory threw back his head and laughed. "Oh my God, he won't wake up for a week and they'll send him back to Sing Sing where he came from . . . I'll miss the bastard." And after a minute, "No, he'll miss me."

"Go back while there's time," Laura pleaded. At the intersection, she made a right turn, again the tires squealed. So did the brakes of a car coming on behind her. She had run the stop sign and cut in front of him. He was not going to be able to stop. She all but lifted the Honda into the left lane, in the path, but at a distance she could handle, of an approaching car. The car behind zoomed past on the passenger's side, his horn blasting. He started to stop and then went on. Laura cruised back into the lane behind him.

"Tim's wrong," the old man said. "It's a darling car."

They were both silent for a time, the road winding and rutted. There was little oncoming traffic, but in the rearview mirror Laura could see a police car approaching. She was of two minds what to do, but before she could settle on one of them, it was too late. The vehicle passed them, its siren sudden and shrill. "Now where are they going?" the old man said.

Laura said nothing. Having slowed down to let them pass,

she had read STATE POLICE CANINE CORPS.

Soon they could see the sky ahead lit up, the color of alarm, of search. The iron fence loomed in the headlights as though rising from the ground. "Now I know," the old man said, and for a few seconds rocked himself in the seat. "Put me down here," he ordered, "and get the hell away."

Laura stopped. The ceiling light came on when he opened the door. He noticed the two boxes of candy on the back seat. "Is one of them for me?"

It was an hour later when Laura stopped near the Massachusetts border, intending to call both Tim and her aunt Mattie. When she went to get money out of her purse, she found the snub-nosed gun. It was of carved wood, polished to a sheen. She also found a small roll of dollar bills tightly bound with a rubber band.